THE RELUCTANT ADVENTURES

OF

FLETCHER CONNOLLY

ON THE

INTERSTELLAR RAILROAD

VOLUME 1

SKINT IDJIT

FELIX R. SAVAGE

THE RELUCTANT ADVENTURES OF FLETCHER
CONNOLLY ON THE INTERSTELLAR RAILROAD
VOLUME 1
SKINT IDJIT

First published in the United States of America in 2016 by Knights Hill Publishing.

Cover art by Christian Bentulan
Interior design and layout by Felix R. Savage

ISBN-10:1-937396-20-7
ISBN-13:978-1-937396-20-6

THE RELUCTANT ADVENTURES

OF

FLETCHER CONNOLLY

ON THE

INTERSTELLAR RAILROAD

VOLUME 1

SKINT IDJIT

CHAPTER 1

I know, I know. What can you expect from a ship named the Skint Idjit? People play to type and so do ships, if the number of Marauders and Hellraisers floating around is anything to go by, hole your shielding as soon as look at you, Jesus have mercy. The Milky Way is infested with pirates, and when I have my own planet I will invest in some decent planetary defenses.

But there aren't any pirates on the Beta Aurigae spur of the Interstellar Railroad. There is no one at all, except us. Our backers sent us out here because it is completely fecking unmapped. As in, we are the first human beings to ever set foot in this region of the galaxy. Here Be Dragons …

I wish.

Dragons, now that'd be something we could flog for cash in hand.

So far, we have discovered:

- Seventeen planets scoured to the crust, presumably in all-out wars fought by their late owners
- Six planets abundant in alien lifeforms presenting varying degrees of convergent evolution—nothing bigger, smarter, or more valuable than a rabbit
- And three planets that aren't there anymore. See 'all-out wars of planetary reduction,' advanced level.

1

These wars all happened millions and millions of years ago. The aliens who prosecuted them are extinct. In the year 2066 of our feeble human reckoning, Homo sapiens is the only intelligent species in the galaxy, although I'm not so sure about the intelligent part.

Exhibit A: our pilot, Woolly, a wookie. She's not really a wookie, of course. If there were any living aliens, which there aren't, I'm sure they would not resemble the fond imaginings of George Lucas. It's A-tech-based cosmetic surgery. The DNA for the hair grafts comes from llamas, but the overall effect is convincing, as well as smelly. Woolly is asleep in the pilot's couch beside me right now. She is snoring.

"Woolly?"

Snore, snore.

"Woolly." I nudge her. A louse crawls out of her arm hair. I pinch it between thumb and forefinger, and wipe my fingers on my jeans. "We're coming up on the next planet. You might want to wake up now."

She surfaces, groaning, and pushes her fringe out of her eyes.

On the console, the main optical feed screen shows the view from the nose camera. The Interstellar Railroad stretches away ahead of us, a glimmering double line of pure ghostly energy, joined by ties of the same spooky stuff. No stars are visible. We're rushing through mysteriously folded space at two lightyears an hour, except it's a lot less than that now, because we'll be slowing down as we go around the next loop, to see if there's anything there worth exploring.

"Oh my freaking God," Woolly says. "What's that?"

The words are scarcely out of her mouth when I see it, too. There's some kind of obstruction at the junction in the distance, where we will veer off onto the next loop.

The bridge of the Skint Idjit is always crowded, because a Boeing X-80 is simply not a very large ship. Harriet, Morgan, and some other odds and sods are playing blackjack for chocolate chips at the navigation table. They all rush up to peer over our shoulders. I am in the co-pilot's seat, which I shouldn't be because I am not a pilot. I'm just the chief A-tech scout. But I have worked on the Railroad more or less continuously since I was eighteen, and I say, "Relax. It's only some gandy dancers."

The gandy dancers are the maintenance entities that came with the Interstellar Railroad. They look like small grey humanoids with overgrown heads. Yes, the same buggers that used to sneak around Earth in their flying saucers. It is thought they were trying to determine if we were sentient or not. These ones are standing on the Railroad, right at the junction, waving their tools and bouncing up and down.

No one knows if the gandy dancers are robots, biologicals, automated at a high level, or governed by conditional logic; no one knows where they came from; no one knows if they created the Railroad, or were created along with it; and least of all does anyone know why they bother, after all these millennia. But it is clear to any sentient being that they are telling the Skint Idjit, "NOT THIS WAY!"

"Woolly, they don't want us to go down the loop," I say. "Maybe we'd better not."

This should not be my decision, it should be the Captain's. He's standing behind me, breathing noisily through the grille of his exoskeleton. He has taken to clanking around in this exoskeleton all the time. He bought it on Arcadia a few months ago. It's A-tech, very advanced, but it makes it hard to tell what he's thinking, especially when he's not saying anything.

We rush closer to the junction, and now I see what's got the gandy dancers in a tizzy. Just beyond the junction, on the local loop, there is a hole in the Railroad.

A hole in the Interstellar Railroad.

Some ties are missing on either side of it, too. The ends of the track look uneven. Chewed.

"Woolly!" I say sharply. "We'll keep going as we were!"

But she doesn't move. She's frozen up completely. Her hairy hands grip the armrests of her couch.

Behind me, everyone's yelling in terror. The Skint Idjit zooms into the junction. The gandy dancers spring out of our way. I lean across Woolly, grab the yoke, and throw it over hard—

—too late.

We hurtle onto the local loop.

So all I've accomplished is to steer us against the curvature of the loop, which is a big no-no, and we fly off the Railroad, just short of the hole in the tracks, into the orbital space of Planet No. 27.

The whine of the chain dogs cuts out. The nuclear thermal drive we use for in-system maneuvering kicks in with its own whooshing hum.

Woolly screams, "What is that?"

"There's nothing there," I shout, which is not exactly true. Planet No. 27 is there. It's just not in one piece. It's in about a million pieces. A new twist on the old 'wars of planetary reduction' theme. The bright bluish-tinged light of a G-type main-sequence star flashes upon continent-sized shards, some of them drifting horribly close to the Skint Idjit. I keep my grip on the yoke and steer us back towards the Railroad, praying I won't smash us into anything.

"Attitude control thrusters," yells the Captain, reacting at last, and not before time. His armored torso crushes me sideways as he leans between our seats to reach the controls.

"It's eating the Railroad!" Woolly squeals.

She's pointing at the infrared display, and it does look like there's something there. Fields of heat, like fluttering wings, embrace the ragged ends of the gap in the Railroad.

On the optical display, gandy dancers scramble over the same area, laying new ties, so maybe the infrared's just picking them up, although I've never seen it do that before.

No time to think about it. I grab Woolly's hands and place them on the yoke, snarling at her to do her job, and then I roll onto the floor so the Captain can take my seat. He can't sit down very easily in that exoskeleton, so he stays on his feet, leaning over the thruster controls.

A thunderous boom resounds through the ship. Everyone screams. Penelope speaks over the intercom from the control deck, as calm as always. "We just sustained damage to the heat rejection system. I'm shutting down the main turbines."

"We're hit we're fecking hit!" shout several people, diving for the door out of the bridge. I don't bother to move off the floor. If we're hit, we're finished. That's all.

"I'd like Saul to visually confirm shutdown of turbines two through eight," Penelope says. "I can keep the reactor running for a few minutes without blowing us all up. Can we get back on the Railroad quickly, though?"

This concentrates Woolly's mind. She pilots us back to the local loop on the far side of the gap, avoiding the nearest pieces of Planet No. 27. Once we're back on the Railroad, we shut down the reactor completely and switch the secondary systems over to battery power. Saul, our main propulsion guy, and his assistants toil on the engineering deck, while I direct some of the scouts to spacewalk and find out how bad the hull damage is. It can't be that bad, as we're still breathing.

I sit at the navigation table amidst the detritus of the blackjack school and drink a coffee with a good-sized dram of whiskey in it.

Morgan sits opposite me and fiddles with the gunnery computer he bought second-hand on Arcadia.

"Morgan?" I say.

"Yeah?"

That should be yes, sir, as Morgan is the leader of Scout Group B, which makes me his boss, but he's the cousin of a friend from Ennis, so we don't stand on ceremony. Actually, on the Skint Idjit, basic manners are in short supply, never mind formality. Morgan is in his boxers and undershirt, and I'm not wearing much more myself.

"You don't need to do that," I tell him.

"I just need to get the optical feed to synchronize with the targeting software."

"And if you did, that piece-of-shite antimatter cannon you bought from the mob would probably explode the first time you fired it. We don't need it out here, Morgan. We're the only human beings within two kiloparsecs."

"Something hit us, if you noticed," he says.

"That wasn't a slug, it was a piece of Planet Number Twenty-fecking-Seven. And if it had been a larger piece, we wouldn't be sitting here."

"I'd still rather be safe than sorry," he says obstinately.

I know the feeling. I eat some chocolate chips left on the table. What Morgan doesn't understand is that if there were any bad guys out here, which there aren't, thank God, his pathetic second-hand antimatter cannon would just give them a laugh at our expense, before they blew us away with their twenty-gun high-energy laser broadside.

My uncle Finian used to have terawatt-class laser batteries on his ship, when I worked for him on the Draco spur. That was twenty years ago, but I can still see the explosions vividly in my memory. It was actually less horrible that way, when there weren't any bodies to bury ... or not bury, as the case might be, because it was more important to make a quick getaway with the A-tech.

There was loads of A-tech on the Draco spur in those days. But now it's all been found and the pirates have to search further afield, running ahead of the tsunami of big money that's sweeping through the exploration industry. So there is a silver lining to Wall Street taking over the industry, bringing in rules and regulations and lawsuits that'll bleed you out as surely as a bullet wound. I may complain about our backers but I'd rather deal with them than with pirates like my uncle. That's another way of saying I'd rather be alive than dead.

Saul calls up from the engineering deck. "Good news," he says. "We can fix the heat rejection system. Bad news, it's going to take a while. I hope the next planet is nice."

"At this point," I tell him, "I'd settle for it being there."

It is there. Eighteen hours after our hasty departure from Planet No. 27, another junction comes in view and we zoom smoothly onto the local loop that encircles Planet No. 28.

From orbit, it's half black and half striped.

The stripe is a band of green around the terminator. The middle of the dayside, facing Planet No. 28's sun, is dry-roasted rock.

"Tidally locked," sighs the Captain. "But where there's green stuff, there's air and water. We'll put down in the twilight zone." He touches the intercom with a metal-gloved finger. "Penny, is it safe to bring the reactor online for a de-orbit burn?"

Even if Penelope said no, we'd have to try it anyway. We need air and water. My fingers close around the old plastic rosary in my pocket.

"Harriet," says the Captain through the grille at the bottom of his faceplate, turning to our life-support officer, "it is your turn to name this newly discovered planet."

"Oh no it's not," says Hendrik, one of my scout group leaders. He's South African, and always suspects us of not giving him a fair shake. "It's my turn. Hers was last planet."

"It was," the Captain acknowledges, "but that was not strictly speaking a planet. So she gets to name this one."

"He can have it," Harriet says. "I hate tidally locked planets." Harriet is supposed to be one of our most stalwart crew members, but I have suspected for some time that she has had enough and would like to go home.

"Ah, go on, Harry," the Captain wheedles.

"Fine." Harriet sighs noisily. "I name this planet Suckass."

CHAPTER 2

As tidally locked planets go, Suckass turns out to be not so bad. It's a little massier than Earth, a little smaller. Its star is a cool dwarf only a bit bigger than Jupiter. The twilight zone, a thousand kilometers wide, goes all the way around the planet. Its ecosystem runs to complex metazoans, what we in the industry call 'animals.' There is no sign that sentient life ever evolved here. The terrain around our LZ is mountainous and covered with photosynthetic organisms ('plants') that look like hundred-foot geraniums with black leaves and green flowers. It's a bit windy.

Despite the superficially unpromising nature of a planet covered (well, at least partly covered) with gargantuan geraniums, I've deployed the scouts to have a look around. They've been gone two days now, and have been in intermittent radio contact. We toasted a kilometer-wide patch of jungle when the *Idjit* landed, leaving the ground knee-deep in charred biomass, which is still blowing away in dusty flurries. Not my idea of a pleasant campsite, so I hauled our stuff to the treeline—doing Harriet's job for her—and set up a nice little bivouac in the shade of the geraniums. As long as you aren't in direct sunlight, the heat is nice.

In fact, for those of us not working on the damaged ship, it feels almost like a holiday. We were certainly due one.

I am kicking back in my hammock on Day 3 when Ruby comes to pester me.

"Any word from the scouts?"

I look up reluctantly from my iPad. Jacob Ruby is six foot three with a hipster beard and pencil biceps. His official title is Deputy A-Tech Scout, which would make him my assistant, but in reality he's a spy foisted upon the *Skint Idjit* by Goldman Sachs, our primary backers. They suspect us of squirrelling away the good stuff and selling it on Arcadia or Flea Market. It has not been easy to convince them that we just have bad luck, but maybe this time out will do it.

"The scouts have found nothing except geraniums," I say. "Oh, I was forgetting. One of them was attacked by a butterfly the size of an eagle."

"Whoa!" says Ruby in his puppyish way, which fools no one. "Got pics?"

"If you want to look in the surface comms archives, I'm sure you'll find plenty of pics in there."

Instead of going away, as I hoped, Ruby drags over a camp stool and sits down beside my hammock. "Whatcha looking at?"

I swiftly close the tab. He already thinks I am up to something. Let him think it has something to do with this footage. Red Herrings 'R' Us. "Nothing," I say with a big smile.

"Aw, c'mon, Fletch."

When I have my own planet, it will be *Mister Connolly* to annoying hipsters like this one. Or maybe *King Fletcher*. Yes, I like the sound of that.

"Porn? I'm not gonna judge you."

There will be no hipsters on my planet, though. There will not be another living soul. Just me and my planetary defenses.

"It's probably *Full Metal Jacket,*" shouts Harriet from behind the tents. "Fletch is a romantic."

I *am* a romantic. My favorite film ever is *Everest V,* that docudrama about the fella who claimed a snow-covered planet and survived there alone for fifteen years. Pure art, although I could do without the snow.

"All right, Ruby, see what you make of this."

He scoots closer. The legs of his camp stool sink into the leaf mulch, a deep layer the consistency of clay, undisturbed by any sentient being for the last trillion years or so.

"This is where we derailed," I say. "Nose cam footage."

You can see the junction, where the local loop of Planet No. 27 curls off from the main spur, and the gandy dancers jumping around on it. I slow the replay. The gandy dancers spring out of the way in slow motion. We glide onto the local loop. In reality, it was sickeningly fast.

"And this is where I grabbed the controls."

Our viewpoint pitches to the right. Then we go into a disorienting tumble. A G-type star flashes at us, occulted every few seconds by large objects that will turn out to be pieces of Planet No.27.

"You're a crap pilot, Fletch," says Harriet, who has meandered over to watch.

"OK, I think we've seen enough of *that.*" I rewind and freeze-frame at the instant before we derail, when we are as close as we'll get to the damaged stretch of track. "This is what I'm interested in. Look at the track."

"Looks pretty chewed up," Ruby says.

"Give the lad a gold star. It does look fairly chewed up. And I'm wondering how a bit of rock could do that much damage."

"Well," says Ruby, "I guess it was a big rock."

"Kinetic energy is proportionate to velocity. Those fragments aren't moving very fast. They're just floating around inside the local loop of the Railroad."

"Well, they holed *us.*"

Apparently losing interest, Ruby wanders away.

"Yeah," I shout after him, "but that's apples and oranges. The *Skint Idjit* is a spaceship. The Interstellar Railroad is an A-tech artifact of unknown provenance, which scientists believe to be constructed of pure energy, having the function of folding spacetime in its immediate vicinity, so it's got to be a bit stronger than a Boeing X-80, wouldn't you say?"

"Yeah man, I guess," is Ruby's response, as he vanishes into his tent.

"I wonder how smart you have to be to act that stupid," I say to Harriet, quite loudly. Ruby really does annoy the shite out of me.

She yawns. "Let's go see how they're getting on with the repairs."

We squelch to the edge of the treeline. Standing in the shade of an awning-sized leaf, we gaze at the *Skint Idjit*. She is a blended-wing atmosphere-capable spaceship, 1000 feet long from nose to thrusters. Claws stick out from her undercarriage like a row of teats, between her landing gear. Those are her chain dogs, energy converters which hook onto the Railroad when we go interstellar. Most of the rest of the ship is the nuclear drive for in-system maneuvering. Hidden away in the middle, behind three-meter-thick shielding, is 6,000 cubic feet of pressurized cabin space ... for 28 of us. It gets quite fetid in there after a few weeks or months, and I'm happy to see both airlocks are open, airing the ship out.

The tiny figures of the Captain, Woolly, and one of Saul's assistants dot the *Idjit's* towering sides. The Captain is wearing his exoskeleton. The others are stripped to the waist like construction workers. They are patching the holes left by microscopic pieces of Planet No. 27. Saul, Penelope, and Saul's other assistant are working on the reactor.

Low in the mustard-colored sky, the dull red disk of Suckass's star subtends an angle of 25 degrees—approximately 50 times the size of the sun as seen from Earth. A thin black line skims the top edge of the disk, bisecting the sky from horizon to horizon. This is the local loop of the Interstellar Railroad. Every connected planet has one.

"I wonder where it came from," Harriet muses.

Of course, nobody knows the answer to that. The Railroad simply zoomed into our solar system one day in 2024, built loops around Earth and Mars, and zoomed onwards to connect the rest of the Orion Arm. Humanity's initial reaction to the Railroad was to attempt to blow it up. This proves that Ruby has shite for brains. An artifact that couldn't be damaged by nukes is not going to get holed by a few bits of rock. Anyway, when we got over our annoyance and terror, we realized there was a galaxy out there to explore.

500 billion stars …

400 billion planets …

40 billion of those Earthalikes (very broadly speaking) in the habitable zone …

And at least 30 billion of those *already* connected by the Railroad.

We seem to have come along rather late in the day, on the galactic timescale.

But it's not so bad.

Because everywhere we go, everyone is dead.

All the countless other civilizations that once flourished in the Milky Way galaxy are history.

And as they say, you can't take it with you. Enough A-tech has already been recovered from once-inhabited worlds to fund Earth's booming exploration industry several times over.

It's nice to be fashionably late.

Earth is teeming with squintillionaires, we've planted colonies on dozens if not hundreds of worlds, the discoverers of new A-tech wonders are feted in the media every week, and all it would take for me to become one of those success stories is one little find.

I uncap my thermos and take a swig of Pepsi, ice-cold despite the eighty-degree heat. Some lucky bastard discovered an alien corpse that was still cold to the touch, despite reposing on a planet whose sun had expanded into a red giant. The body bag on that corpse proved to be reverse-engineerable, and said lucky bastard now has his own planet.

That's all it would take.

One little tiny find that isn't shite.

Harriet says, "Do you think Ruby guesses about the treecats?"

The treecats *are* shite. We picked them up on Planet No.14, Lisdoonvarna XV (named by the Captain). They're now in a pressurized inflatable animal habitat in the cargo hold. They're not going to fetch much, so there is no need to let our backers know about them. One-fortieth of not much is better than one-fortieth of fifty percent of not much. But even if they catch on as pets, it's not going to buy me a planet, is it?

"Bugger the treecats," I say.

"Oh come on, you like them," Harriet says, without conviction. She starts walking into the sunlight. "I'm going to make sure they've been fed. The Captain said he would do it while he's up there, but I bet he'll forget."

I watch her walk towards the ship, scuffing up charred geranium leaves like a little girl at the beach. Harriet has shapely hips, and it's a nice view. I muse that this is probably the best view obtainable on Suckass. We are 2.3 kiloparsecs from home.

The wind drops for a minute, as it sometimes does, and the world goes so quiet that I can hear Harriet's footsteps crunching in the ashes. I also hear the Captain's groan of despair when he drops his carbon-foam applicator. It thuds to the ground 60 feet below. He always was bad with his hands. Cut off the top of his own pinky finger in fabrication class when we were first-years.

My radio squelches. I jump, startled.

"Fletch here."

"Help!" yells the person on the other end. I hold the radio away from my face and frown at it.

"What did you say?"

"HELP!"

"Who is this?" It's one of the scouts but he hasn't identified himself.

"This is Morgan. Get off your arse, you dosser, we need HELP! It's eaten Eamon and Aisling!"

"What?"

A wordless wail from Morgan, and the radio goes dead.

Well.

That doesn't sound good.

Ruby's face floats pale in the shade under the geraniums. "Everything OK, Fletch?"

"They've got a problem," I say, bringing up the GPS screen on my radio. We dropped a handful of sats in orbit on our way down. Each explorer has a beacon that pinpoints his or her location.

"What kind of problem?"

"At a guess, a complex metazoan problem."

Holy feck. Morgan is on the nightside. In fact, the whole of Scout Group B is on the nightside, about a mile past the terminator.

Before my eyes, their little red location bubbles vanish.

"Now they've turned off their beacons." I record their last known coordinates and trudge towards the tents to pick up some stuff.

A ghastly scream spins me around.

The Captain has come off the ship, exoskeleton and all. I am just in time to see him hit the ground.

Harriet breaks into a run.

That wasn't the Captain screaming. It was her.

"He's fallen!" Ruby shouts. "Is he hurt?"

I'm starting to believe this one really is as stupid as he acts. "He'll be fine. That's what the fecking exoskeleton is for. Impact protection, rad protection, you-name-it protection."

Harriet reaches the Captain. She screams again.

Ruby charges past me, arms windmilling. I pick up my pace a bit.

Lying on the ground, covered with ash, the Captain in his exoskeleton looks like an actual skeleton of some long-dead alien. I shove everyone else aside and rattle my knuckles on the exoskeleton's fishbowl helmet. Inside, his face is as red as a tomato. There must be a way to open this piece of shite from the outside.

There isn't.

Saul fetches a power saw.

I move away and radio Scout Group A. "How are you doing, Lukas? Listen, Morgan and his crew are in a spot of trouble … yeah, I know." Scout Group A are 1,238 miles from Scout Group B's last known location. But Scout Group C are even further away. "Well, the sooner you get airborne, the sooner you'll be there, won't you?"

The power saw sings. I stick my finger in my free ear. Lukas Sakashvili, the leader of Scout Group A, quacks at me about having to finish recharging their batteries before they can go anywhere. He's *so* committed to health and safety, it warms my heart.

"He's not responding," shouts Harriet, who doubles as the ship's medic.

"Just go," I yell at Sakashvili, and turn off the radio.

The Captain is dying from heatstroke.

He overheated in that fecking exoskeleton.

Harriet and Saul ride up with him in the bucket of the *Skint Idjit's* cargo winch. The stairs are broken, so we're reduced to using the cargo winch to get in and out of the ship. Rapid cooling is the Captain's only chance of avoiding organ failure and death. We have A-tech coming out of our ears, and yet all we can do for him is pop him in the freezer. I feel like I'm stuck in the 18th century.

We all stand around watching the cargo winch rise into the air until it docks with the airlock. The streamlined nose of the *Skint Idjit* cuts a black wedge out of the grotesquely oversized sun.

"Right. I've got to be off," I say to no one in particular. "I'm sure you can handle this."

Woolly gawps at me. "Where are you going?"

"A minor issue with one of the scout groups," I say, aware of Ruby watching me with narrowed eyes. *He* overheard Morgan shouting for help. The hell with him. "I'm taking my flitter. I should be back by this time tomorrow."

We are much closer to Morgan's location than Scout Group A are. They will dawdle, anyway. Haste would not comport with their keen commitment to 'elf 'n' safety *(theirs,* not anyone else's).

"You don't need me here, do you?" I say, already turning away.

Donal O'Leary, the Captain and owner of the *Skint Idjit,* is my oldest friend. We grew up together in County Clare. Shoplifting from Lidl, drinking lager down the marina, breaking into the trade school to print out model spaceships of our own design … we had good craic. But it's a long long way from Clare to here, as the man sang. And there is no denying the Captain has been slipping recently. The exoskeleton; his refusal to come out of it—he's been *sleeping* in the fecking thing; Jesus, he even complimented Woolly on her flying the other day, and that's when I knew he'd lost it.

The right stuff is like anything else, you see. It trickles away over time.

One day you wake up and you just can't do it anymore.

I'll be dead before that happens to me.

So I collect my stuff and wedge it into the pod of the last remaining flitter, and I take off into the wind, and I waggle my wings at the people below. Then I zoom away to the west. Cheeky auld Fletch.

CHAPTER 3

The flitters are great little vehicles. A-tech, of course, from the same find that gave us flying cars, at bloody last, and turned every morbidly obese person and decrepit pensioner on Earth into a levitating menace to society. It's a complete crapshoot, isn't it? You can't control what people find and no more can you control what people do with it.

But you *can* cash in, and as I fly west that is what I am planning to do.

Whatever Morgan's group has found, it must be fairly impressive. Our scouts carry energy weapons that could stop a tank.

Am I not in the least worried about getting eaten, mauled, or otherwise embuggered myself?

Nah.

I am 99% sure that Morgan was taking the piss. If he was *really* in trouble, he'd have triggered his emergency beacon, instead of switching off his locator beacon to boot. "It's eaten Eamon and Aisling"—not sure what he was on about there, but if it's serious, I've got my lightsaber, anyway.

My mind fills with visions of caverns packed with A-tech, hidden away on the nightside of Suckass. The secret of eternal life. Toothbrushes that never get bits of food stuck in them. Dog hair repellent. A non-broken version of that duplicator found five years ago on Seventh Heaven—that's what all the backers are after right now. Dragons.

I zoom over endless ridges and valleys covered with geraniums. Their black coloration makes the shadow of my flitter invisible, except when I pass above a patch of green flowers. The flitter is about the size of a Cessna 120, except with twice the wingspan. The wings are solar panels, which recharge the battery of the flitter's anti-grav engine as I fly.

Presently I see something queer: a pale patch in the geraniums.

Snapping out of my dreams of riches beyond the wildest, etc., I fly down for a closer look. The patch is roughly circular and measures half a mile across. It is a *bald* patch. Well, almost bald. It is covered with baby geraniums.

It looks an awful lot like our LZ.

Or rather, like our LZ will look some weeks or months after we leave.

Dark suspicions clouding my mind, I set the flitter down near the edge of the bald patch. The wheels crush the new growth, releasing a pungent scent. The baby geraniums are knee high. How fast do they grow? Feck knows, but let's say an inch a week.

It has been about five months since someone else's spaceship landed here, charring out an LZ for itself, just like we did.

I turn my face up to the sullen, bloated sun and curse our backers, 2.3 kiloparsecs away.

Never before visited, they said. Completely unmapped, they said. You'll be the first, they said. You've every chance of finding something new.

" A little bit of oppo research would have helped!"

Unless—darker suspicions—they've covertly backed *another* ship and pointed it in the same direction, to double their chances of finding whatever there is here to find.

Viciously, I hope there's nothing on this spur *to* find. Misery loves company.

I kick through the baby geraniums for a while, to punish the stubborn part of my brain that still doesn't want to believe the bad news. It only takes a few minutes before I find a crisp packet, its colors still vivid. Filthy litterers. Then, investigating the treeline, I find some forgotten washing hanging from a stem. Several pairs of boxer shorts, some A-tech socks (they never get stinky!), and a pair of Carhartt bib overalls. I am tempted to take the overalls for myself, but principle supervenes.

This is not really much of a clue, as everyone in the exploration industry wears Carhartt, Wranglers, Dickies, etc.

But I'll definitely be having a word with Ruby when I get back.

I go back to the flitter to use the radio. "Morgan? Come in, Morgan." He needs to know about this.

He doesn't answer.

Feck. What if he really is in trouble?

What if the owners of this washing are still on Suckass— and *they've* found him?

A gauzy shadow falls across the flitter. Clouds blot out the sun. It's time for Suckass to do its one and only party trick: pouring down with rain.

Now slightly more concerned about the fate of Morgan's group, I decide to fly straight through it. Neither our instruments nor our own eyes have picked up any signs of electrical storms on Suckass, so I'm not at risk of getting hit by lightning. What's a little water?

Actually, a metric fucktonne of water.

Eh, screw it. I'm Irish.

I make it through the storm without problems, but by the time the sun comes out again, my battery is redlining. That's the trouble with the flitters. Anti-grav gobbles juice. As I fly onwards, the solar panels on the wings feed electricity straight to the engine, with none left over to top up the battery. The situation is so marginal that I daren't use the heater, and I'm now so close to the terminator that it is bloody cold up here. I switch on the radio.

The flitter promptly sinks lower in the sky.

"Morgan? Morgan, come in."

No joy.

"*Idjit,* this is Fletch, any change?"

"He hasn't woken up yet," Woolly says. Her voice breaks. "I don't think he's going to."

My flitter is practically brushing the tops of the geraniums. "Got you, Woolly. Well, tell Harriet to do her best."

I have to switch off the radio then or crash. The flitter labors back into the sky, and I see the terminator.

Everything ahead just sort of fades into twilight.

I'd like to take the flitter across the terminator and check out Morgan's last known coordinates from a safe height, but that is not happening with no battery power.

The scouts have figured out how to land the flitters safely on Suckass. I implement their procedure. It goes like this:

Turn off engine

Gradually damp anti-grav effector

Pray

It works! The flitter's wings come to rest on top of the geraniums, supported by the crowns of three separate plants. The stems creak and bow, but do not give way.

I scramble out onto the port wing, hung about with stuff like a donkey, and walk along it to the nearest geranium. Conscious that I'm 80 feet up, and mindful of what happened to the Captain, I rope on and descend to the forest floor.

The geraniums are widely enough spaced that I can look up and see the flitter resting like a giant insect on the flowers. I'll let it sit there and recharge until I come back. There's definitely something to be said for a planet where it is always day.

Except where it is always night.

I trudge between the geraniums, periodically stopping to knock leaf muck off my boots, until there are no more geraniums. In their place grows a weird kind of purple grass. Adapted to the deep twilight zone, it's a whole separate ecosystem.

The grass has broad blades with sharp edges. I'm glad I'm wearing thick jeans. The warm wind blowing from behind me ruffles the grass in waves, so I seem to be up to my waist in purple water. I glance back. I don't see anyone. But that means nothing, and I'm a sitting duck, here in the open.

I slide my lightsaber out of its holster. I've not wielded it in anger in twenty years, but streaks are made to be broken. If it turns out that our backers have screwed us, and Morgan's in trouble as a result, *angry* won't begin to cover it.

The grass fades from purple to gray as I walk towards the darkness. Puffball butterflies flutter around. One of them lands on my arm and tries to take a piece out of me. It has a proboscis the size of a robin's beak.

"Shoo!"

"Fletch?"

The shout comes out of the darkness.

"Morgan?" I start to run, the grass slicing at my jeans.

"Ah, thank Christ you're here." His voice is weak. "It's a

nightmare, Fletch, it's a fecking disaster."

Morgan's a real piss artist. But I've known him for a long time and I've never heard him sound like this.

"Morgan, where are you?"

"Over here."

I run towards his voice. It's getting darker. I pull my torch off my utility belt and switch it on.

"Turn that shite off!"

I nearly step on Morgan. He is lying in the grass. It's only low, patchy tufts here, almost beyond the reach of the light. He grabs weakly at my torch.

"Turn it off!"

"Jesus God, Morgan, what happened to you?"

He is gray. His face looks drained and haggard. He seems to have shrunk inside his clothes. I can't see a scratch on him, but it's clearly not mere exhaustion that has felled him, it's something worse. I start thinking about bacteria, alien viruses, fatal infections. You'll have every chance of finding something new, they said. Something that's never been found before.

"Would you turn that fecking torch off?"

I do as he asks. In the deep twilight I take a knee beside him. "First of all tell me, is it contagious?"

"I had my immune booster last month."

These immunization shots we get are A-tech. Humanity's first journeys to alien planets were complete carnage, valiant explorers snuffing it left and right, whole crews suiciding to keep the alien bugs from getting back to Earth. Then you had a period when explorers were shuffling around in EVA suits à la Neil Armstrong. Surface rats, they called them, or white rats. Very humorous. *Then* someone found this all-purpose immune booster, and here we are today, sat on Suckass in our shirtsleeves.

Aren't we the lucky ones.

"It's not a fecking bug, Fletch. It's wildlife. Or more likely A-tech."

"Did you get any—"

"No, I didn't stop to take any pictures while it was *eating Aisling's FACE!*"

This roar of self-justifying rage is Morgan's last. His face goes slack. He falls backwards. His head bounces off the ground, and comes to rest at a sideways angle. His mouth hangs open.

My mouth hangs open, too. I stare at him, completely gob-smacked.

Pulling myself together, I check his vital signs, but there's no point really. I can see he's dead.

I stand up and point my lightsaber into the darkness. If anything pounces out at me, I'll scream and run.

Nothing happens for several minutes. My arm starts to ache.

I walk away a bit to use my portable radio. I'm using the flitter's more powerful transmitter to re-broadcast my signal. "Lukas? … Yeah, you might want to hurry it up. Yes … Maybe … No, he's dead. I don't know. Just fecking get here."

When I end the conversation, I realize how stupid I've been, walking away from Morgan to talk, as if he were asleep and I didn't want to wake him up.

I go back to his body. It is covered with puffball butter-flies.

"Get off him, you wee buggers!"

Where they've been feeding from the corpse—basically, on every bit of exposed skin—it looks shrivelled. *Vampire* butterflies. What a lovely planet this is, to be sure.

CHAPTER 4

Eight hours later, Scout Group A finds me still sitting beside Morgan's body, shooing the butterflies away.

"Hell! You OK, boss?" Sakashvili says.

"I'm OK. He's not."

"The rest of them?"

"Somewhere over there." I stand up. Ow, my back is stiff. Sakashvili gives me a look that holds me responsible for whatever has happened to Morgan's crew, and for whatever will happen to Sakashvili's own crew when they follow, under fervent protest, my undoubtedly feckless and half-arsed orders.

They have disembarked from their flitters in biohazard suits, hung about with weapons and specimen packs and all the bells and whistles. "Good job you brought that stuff," I say approvingly.

I'm *trying*, see? Praise people when they do something right. Management 101.

Then Sakashvili opens his mouth and I just know the next thing out of it will be something about health and safety.

I snap, "Give me that," and I jerk at the seals of his biohazard suit. He howls as I pull it off him. I think his terror is genuine, although he doesn't try to stop me from taking his bunny suit. He is more terrified of me right now than of imaginary alien bugs. Can you believe this man hails from the same city that gave us Stalin? *I* believe it. They're religious about 'elf 'n' safety, these Slavs. I suppose it's because the concept is new to them, historically speaking.

That said, Sakashvili has other points in his favor.

I put on his bunny suit and tell him, "Wait here."

He will wait. He will wait until night comes and the atmosphere freezes. Because Sakashvili would sell his soul for a sniff of A-tech, and so would his cousins and his friends' aunties' neighbors (the lads grouped behind him in a fluorescent yellow huddle). The Irish are not the only ones who consider nepotism a virtue.

Donal and Morgan, both gone in a single day.

Walking into the darkness, I shake a bit.

I'm the only one of our group left now.

Mother of God, but the universe is an unfriendly place.

The air's getting colder. I start to shiver, even inside the biohazard suit, which usually makes you sweat like a pig. Worse, it's slippery underfoot and I have to watch my footing.

I can hardly see a fecking thing now. In a harebrained spasm of defiance, I switch my torch onto the highest power setting. The 1,000,000 candle-power beam stabs into the dark ahead of me.

Yes, I know Morgan said to switch it off, but he was clearly wandering in his wits.

The beam illuminates black rock glistening with moisture. A bright red object flies past me. I nearly shoot it before I realize it's just a bandanna, carried on the tepid wind from the dayside. In fact, it's the same one Aisling used to wear.

I run after it and trap it under my boot. For some reason this little find convinces me that Aisling, Eamon, and the other three members of Morgan's crew are dead.

I am tying the bandanna around my wrist when the night

rushes towards me.

It's a storm of flailing darkness, a blast of colder air, a stink of dusty fur, and I act on sheer instinct.

I throw my torch at it.

In the follow-through of the same movement I am aiming my lightsaber, and I have time to sight on the monster because it's actually stopped. It is stroking my torch with its wingtips, doting on it, and no I'm not imagining this, it *does* have wings. About six hundred of them. It is in fact one of those bleeding puffball butterflies. A Godzilla-sized version.

Well, maybe not quite that big.

But it is definitely as big as an eagle.

Wisps of steam tear from between its wings. The steam looks ghostly in the light of the torch that's lying on the ground, shining up into the furry crevices of the thing.

And then the torch starts to dim.

I stab Butterfly-zilla with my lightsaber.

This lightsaber is not exactly like the ones they used to wave around in the Star Wars movies. It has much better range, for one thing. But it's similar enough that I feel justified calling it that.

It's A-tech, of course. It shoots laser pulses at the rate of one per femtosecond, so that they appear to converge into a solid blue beam as thick as your arm.

Luke Skywalker, eat your heart out.

"Die motherfecker die die die!" I scream at the top of my lungs.

Butterfly-zilla does not die. It perks up. It clusters its forewings together and stretches them *into* the beam, like a person might stretch out their cold hands to a fire. Abandoning my torch, it flutters heavily towards me, and the more I shoot it the faster it comes, the wet-dog stink of its wings filling my nostrils, and all I can think of to do is mash the pushbutton even harder, and its wings curve around to embrace me and the lightsaber together, and at the last possible minute a new idea comes to me.

Actually it's the same idea I had to begin with, before I got carried away with the thought of avenging my friends.

Scream and run.

I don't bother with the screaming part. I just release the pushbutton of the lightsaber and take to my heels.

Running, I wrench things off my utility belt and toss them behind me, in hopes that it will slow Butterfly-zilla down. After all, that seemed to work with the torch.

The camera. The iPad. The radio. All my various A-tech analysis gadgets. Away they go, one after the other, bouncing into the dark.

But it's not working, or not working well enough.

I can *smell* Butterfly-zilla catching up. I can hear its wings beating, a noise like a thousand paper bags being crumpled. Something bats lightly at the back of my bunny-suited head, and I put on a new burst of speed.

Stumbling, my lungs on fire, I see mustard-yellow daylight.

Sakashvili's crew crowd towards me, clustering at the edge of the grassy zone like a bunch of children afraid to go into the water.

Why aren't *they* running?

Because they can't see Butterfly-zilla. The bloody thing is as black as the devil's underpants. You'd never know it was there until it got you. That's how Morgan's crew must have died.

I throw one last item behind me, and Butterfly-zilla's wing-beats fade.

Completely out of breath, I stagger into the grass and collapse. Knife-like pains stab my lungs. My heart feels like it will burst. I'm only forty-two, and I'd have said I was fit, but I think I've just broken the galactic record for sprinting in Timberlands.

Sakashvili & Co. pelt me with panicky questions. Still fighting for breath, I haul myself upright and stare into the darkness.

"Lukas," I say to Sakashvili. "Do you recall on Day One, you reported an attack from a butterfly the size of an eagle?"

"Yeah. Is *that* what kill Morgan?"

"Yeah." Poor fecking Morgan. He didn't run faster than Butterfly-zilla. He ran faster than everyone else. But it wasn't enough to save him.

Shuddering, I rub my gloved hands down the sides of my biohazard suit. I didn't outrun Butterfly-zilla, either. But I had this.

"What was the Butterfly-zilla that attacked you doing at the time?"

"The what?"

"The fecking butterfly! That attacked you!"

"You want coordinates?"

"Yes!"

"Oh, it was on nightside. But no big deal," Sakashvili says. "We were maybe 300 meters up. It fly into engine of Uznadze's flitter. Nearly break the shit thing. Insect fall down to ground, dead as fuck, and he have to do emergency landing in grass like this."

"Was that on account of battery problems?"

"Yeah, that battery still don't hold charge. He use spare now. I told you about this. Why?"

"Give me your torch!"

30

I make sure the torch is on the *lowest* power setting. Then I walk warily, one step at a time, back the way I came. At the edge of the grassy strip, I realize the Georgians are not following me.

I go back and roar at them a bit. The end result is Sakashvili still refuses to come, because he hasn't got a bunny suit. I'm wearing it. That's OK. He can stay with Morgan. This charmer Uznadze goes first, with the torch, while I hold someone's camera at the ready.

Not thirty yards into the dark, Uznadze lets out a shocked yell in Russian.

Then he sprints back the way we came, easily breaking my speed record.

I stay where I am, snapping pictures.

In the instant the torch was shining on Butterfly-zilla, I confirmed that it is not moving. It is resting on the rock with its wings all pointing straight up, like, well, like a butterfly.

I'm pretty sure it is busy with the last thing I threw down: the spare powerpack for my lightsaber.

I jog back to Morgan's corpse. The Georgians, ever attentive to regulations, have put him in a body bag. This is exactly what I was hoping for, and I tip him out of it. "Come back, you COWARDLY GOBSHITES!" I yell at their receding figures.

Pride gets the better of them. They trickle back and I snatch Sakashvili's spare powerpack off his belt. "Give me your weapon, too. Your torch. Anything that's got a battery …" I drop the items into the body bag. "Uznadze and you," I can never remember their names, "come with me."

The two men scowl behind their perspex masks, mentally filing their worker's compensation claims, I can see. When I explain what we're going to do, they mentally file their life insurance claims. But they do not mutiny. There's spirit in the old East yet.

Carrying the body bag with the gadgets in it, we trot back into the darkness.

Butterfly-zilla is still enjoying its meal.

"Here, big boy." I lay the body bag down, open at one end. "Here you go, fresh and hot. Come and get it … FECK!"

I forgot how fast Butterfly-zilla can move. In an instant it is on top of us, burrowing into the body bag, pointing all its wings into the closed end where the gadgets are. Jesus but it smells horrible, even through the HEPA filter. I think about my planet and I throw myself on top of it, flattening its wings. It feels like a sackful of ferrets wriggling under me. "Close the zipper, CLOSE IT!"

We get Butterfly-zilla bagged up and lug it back into the daylight. A hysterical cackle bursts out of me.

"If this A-tech material," I say, pointing at the body bag, "can keep a fizzy drink ice-cold in ninety-degree heat, it should be able to contain our fuzzy friend!"

"I don't get it," grumps Sakashvili.

I remove the hood of my bunny suit and drink a gallon of tarragon-flavored lemonade, which is what the Georgians carry around with them. Disgusting stuff. Right now it tastes gorgeous. "These are vampire butterflies." I wave at the wee ones fluttering around us, landing on our bunny suits. "I don't think they're butterflies at all, actually. They look like it to us, because our minds search for Earth analogues. But they're not even organic. They're A-tech."

The Georgians shout hooray. This is a wee bit inappropriate, in my opinion, considering that Morgan's body lies near us, and the bodies of five more of our colleagues lie somewhere beyond the terminator, entombed forever in the icy dark.

"My theory is they feed on electricity," I say. "I stabbed that big fecker with my lightsaber and it drank up the beam. It was like spraying booze down the throat of an alcoholic! I've never seen anything like it! That's the same reason it went for the powerpacks, the torches … *especially* the powerpacks."

These, needless to say, are A-tech. A fist-sized package contains the KW equivalent of a legacy-tech battery the size of a bungalow back on Earth. The discovery that broke the battery bottleneck may have banked more licensing revenue than any other. And I believe we have just discovered its opposite.

The faces of the Georgians fall.

To cheer them up, I add, "They'll drain *anything* that produces electricity. And you know what else does? That's right … the human brain. We have tiny electrical impulses running through our nerves all the time. We're walking feasts for these fellas!"

Sakashvili whacks the butterfly that has just landed on his arm. His face is a sight to behold. The other Georgians, safe in their bunny suits, piss themselves laughing.

"I think it'll take more than that to do any serious damage," I say.

"This useless discovery!" Sakashvili says. "Is shit! Who want A-tech that *drain* electricity? Useless!"

I shake my head. "Have I got to do all the thinking around here? *Shields,* guys. Defenses against energy weapons."

The security situation on the Railroad is awfully unbalanced at the moment. Every claim-jumper and his sidekick commands vast reserves of power, thanks to A-tech batteries, see above. And law-abiding ships like the *Skint Idjit* have no defenses other than shields three yards thick.

Butterfly shields, as I am already thinking of them, will change that forever.

Sakashvili's eyes light up with avarice. He's getting it now. He casts a lustful glance at the body bag.

I sling my arm around his shoulders and walk him away from the others. Suckass's bloated sun peeks over the horizon, spearing red light into our eyes.

In a low voice, I say, "This doesn't have to go any further, Lukas. It can stay between the two of us."

Well, the seven of us. But I know Sakashvili can control his crew. There is a good reason they are such scaredy-cats, apart from taking their cues from him. If they breathe the wrong way, he'll get his contacts in Tbilisi to kneecap their grannies. This is the point about Sakashvili. He's connected.

Myself and Morgan and Donal were going to involve him, anyway, if and when we found anything worth selling.

It's a shame that Morgan is dead, and Donal is languishing at death's door. It's a disaster.

But I can just about persuade myself that it's not an unmitigated disaster, because half of a nine-figure payday is better than a quarter of a nine-figure payday. A *lot* better.

I'll spend some of it on houses and cars for their families. They'll sing my praises all over County Clare.

Sakashvili nods and nods, transfixed. "I arrange auction when we get back to Arcadia," he mutters. "Defense sector, yeah. Maybe also energy sector. I reach out to right guys. All keep quiet." He scowls up at me. "*You* can keep quiet until we reach Arcadia?"

"Sure I can." We are walking in a circle, back to where the others are waiting. "I've got it all planned."

"How you explain Morgan dead? With all crew?"

I drop my arm from his shoulders. "I'll think of something!"

The other Georgians are holding the body bag by its corners. It is jumping as if trying to fly away.

I stride past them to Morgan's corpse. "It doesn't need all of youse to carry that body bag! Someone help me with him." I know it's daft, but I'm not leaving him behind. I just can't.

CHAPTER 5

Morgan's body is stinking to high heaven by the time we get back to the LZ. Yeah, we had spare body bags, but we used all of them to capture more Butterfly-zillas. This has also brought us to the edge, power-wise. The flitters limp home on solar power. All our spare batteries and powerpacks are now dead lumps of A-tech inside the body bags that swing beneath our flitters.

We are met in the LZ by Woolly and Saul, wearing faces of woe. I have been lying my arse off on the radio for the last 24 hours, laying the groundwork for the lies I'm about to tell.

"Gosh, they look so small," sighs Woolly, watching the Georgians manhandle the body bags.

She thinks the body bags contain the corpses of Morgan and his crew. We caught enough Butterfly-zillas to make up the right number. They're heavy enough. They are a bit flat-looking, though.

"Have some respect!" I yell. The Georgians recollect themselves and carry the body bags towards the *Idjit*, one at a time, with the solemnity of undertakers.

"This is a goddamn tragedy," Saul says. *"All* of them!"

"They were mucking around on a glacier," I say sadly. "Roped together, for safety. When the first one went into a crevasse, they all went in."

There really are glaciers on Suckass. That's how the water cycle works. It freezes on the nightside and the tidal bulge pulls it towards the dayside, where it liquefies into mighty rivers. I didn't dispatch any scout groups to the glaciers or the rivers. It is my policy not to order people to do things I would rather do myself, and I quite fancied a dip at some point. Now this has worked out to my benefit, as no one will be able to disprove my story.

When the rivers flow into the baking-hot regions of the dayside, they evaporate and the steam is blown around the planet by the wind. That's where the downpours come from. What does not fall on us falls on the nightside, where it freezes, and around we go for umpty billions of years. I can't wait to get off this planet.

"Our insurance premiums are gonna go through the roof," Saul says.

That is what *he* considers a tragedy. I don't feel guilty at all about leaving him out. Harriet? Her heart isn't in this, anyway. Woolly? She's a wookie—nuff said. I run down the crew list in my mind and confirm that not a single one of them deserves a share of our soon-to-be riches.

But one name jumps out in my mind as deserving something quite different, that is, a punch in the gob, and I say casually, "Where's Ruby?"

"Oh, the schmuck from Goldman Sachs?" Saul says. "He's up there talking to the Captain."

"*What?*"

"What do you mean what?"

"I thought the Captain was dead!"

"Oh no, he's recovering."

"Harriet said he was still in the freezer!"

"Yup. He feels comfortable in there, apparently."

"Jesus." I'm grinning my face off. "Is he fit to travel?"

"In my opinion, yeah, he is," Saul says, and his expression says *But he's not fit for anything else.*

This changes everything. I have to get up there, but I also have to stay down here.

The Georgians are loading the body bags into the cargo winch.

"Sakashvili!" Jogging towards them, I gesture back at the flitters. "Stay here with a few of your lads," I tell him. "Make sure no one goes near … you know. I'll take the bags up."

"Hurry up," he says. "I want to eat." They have been surviving on ration bars and lemonade out in the field.

The winch hoists me and Uznadze and six quiescent Butterfly-zillas into the air. We hump the body bags into the airlock.

The interior of the *Skint Idjit* is as cramped as the caves near Lisdoonvarna, where I grew up. Miles of corridors scarcely wide enough for your shoulders, drips falling on your head from the leaks, litter in the corners. Me and Uznadze load the body bags onto one of the anti-grav cargo dollies and follow it forward to the crew deck.

You have to go through the mess to reach the kitchen. Trigger, our cook, is kneading defrosted dough into loaves. At the sight of the body bags he bows his head and lays one hand on his heart. I feel a bit guilty.

The door to the walk-in freezer is in the corner behind the microwaves. I heave the door open and Uznadze wedges it with the dolly. Cold fog billows out.

"Captain, you're back with us, are you? High time!"

My jocular words mask dismay. The Captain is sitting in his exoskeleton on a cardboard box of frozen food. Ruby stands in front of him. We have obviously interrupted a tense conversation.

"What's your problem, Fletch?" Ruby says crossly.

"I want to store the bodies of our shipmates in here where they won't rot," I say with dignity. Uznadze starts to unload the dolly. I gesture urgently at him to stop. Ruby is staring at the body bags. If he gets a look at them up close, he'll see that the things inside are the wrong size and shape. They don't look at all like corpses really. Bugger, bugger, bugger!

But Ruby's neat little hipster beard is white with frost, and his bare arms are all over gooseflesh. He decides it's not worth hanging out in here any longer. "We can continue this conversation later," he says to the Captain, and strides out without meeting my eyes.

The minute he's gone, I drag the dolly into the freezer, tell Uznadze to keep watch outside, and close the door. "Feck, it's freezing in here," I say heartily.

We're not at risk of getting stuck, anyway—this freezer opens from the inside as well. Health and safety.

I take the Captain's A-tech gloves in my hands and give them a double shake. "How're you feeling, Donal?"

His faceplate is frosted up on the outside and fogged up on the inside, so I can't see his face. His voice emerges hollowly from the grille at the base of the faceplate. "Ah, not too bad."

"You're recovered, anyway? Harriet's given you the green light to resume your duties?"

"Well, that's the trouble," he says.

But I don't let him finish. I'm in too much of a hurry to share my news. "Have they told you Morgan's dead?"

"Yeah. He always was a careless sod. And the others with him?"

"Dead, too."

"Fecking idjits."

"I know."

And that's all we say about it. If you were to think about it too much, let alone talk about it, you'd just go to pieces. So we don't.

I've no clue what the Captain is thinking about inside there, but I know what *I'm* thinking about: nine figures, split three ways between me and the Captain and the Georgians.

"Now for the good news," I say. I heave the first body bag off the dolly. "This isn't Morgan and his crew in here. It's our retirement plan."

When someone's wearing an exoskeleton you can't see how they're taking things. I'd have expected the Captain to be a bit more excited. He says all the right things in response to my story, like "That'll be great," and "We'll have to give some of it to their families," but it seems like his heart's not in it.

I finally take the bull by the horns. "Captain, what's wrong with you?"

"Nothing's wrong with me, fact o' God," he grumps.

The hard work of stacking the body bags, moving boxes and sacks to make room for them in a corner, has warmed me up a bit, but I still can't take much longer in here. "Spit it out, Donal!"

He sighs out a puff of white. "Ruby's trying to kill me."

"Yeah, he's a gobshite. Hang on. Do you mean he's literally trying to kill you?"

"Of course that's what I mean. I'm not living in this bloody thing for my health. It's itchy and I've got a horrible rash from the sweat building up inside. Boils on my arse and everything."

I frown. "Ruby had his chance when you were out with the heatstroke." We cut Donal out of the exoskeleton. I can see where it's been mended, a clumsy weld down the middle of the torso.

"No, he never had a chance. Harriet was hovering over me like a mother hen. She slept on a cot beside me while I was out. I owe my life to that woman."

Well, well. Harriet does her job for once. I move her up on the shortlist for a nice little present once we've sold the A-tech.

"Why is he trying to kill you?" I ask warily. "It can't just be because he's a gobshite."

Another sigh. "Fletch, I didn't want to worry you, but ..."

These are leading candidates for the worst seven words in the English language.

"Me and Penelope have been having problems."

CHAPTER 6

This is bad. This is potentially very bad, but it's not so bad I can't joke about it. "Yet more proof that behind every successful man, there's a woman trying to stab him in the back."

The Captain laughs gloomily at the idea of himself as a successful man, although he is. He's the captain of a fecking exploration ship. When we're home, the local media are all over him. He gets requests to speak at schools and shite.

We never got that treatment when we were starting out. Everyone in County Clare expected us to be dead within the year. There was more awareness then that the Interstellar Railroad is dangerous. Now Wall Street's propaganda has sold it to them as a safe and profitable business opportunity, and they're all waiting—with increasing impatience—for us to bring home the bacon.

But the trouble is it's still dangerous, as we have seen to our cost this day. You can't explain what it's like to the people at home, they don't understand, and I know I've been thinking that the easiest thing would be never to go home again at all.

I will name my planet something like Fletchworld, and there won't be any hypocritical, grasping Irish people on it-- well, apart from me.

I know the stress has been getting to the Captain, too. But

what I didn't know is how he has been coping with it.

I make him tell me exactly what's been going on, and it takes a fair old time in between all the errrs and ummmms and "I know it takes two to tango" and "I'm not saying Penny's in the wrong" (although that is exactly what he's saying). I pace up and down with impatience as much as to stay warm, but by the time I get the picture I've forgotten that I'm freezing my arse off. My rage could melt the dark side of Suckass.

The Captain has been having it off with … drum-roll please … Harriet.

This has been going on since Stig's World, which was five planets before our last visit to Arcadia. So, the best part of a year.

And I never noticed a thing!

You would think there is no privacy on a Boeing X-80 inhabited by 28 people, would you not?

I certainly thought so. Many's the night I've hied me to the bogs for a quiet dump, only to find there's a queue because someone is wanking in there and one of the Georgians is timing him. Har, har. Oh, it's a non-stop party on the *Skint Idjit*, and there are no corners to sneak off to for a fag.

But it's different, obviously, when one of the guilty parties has the luxury of a cabin to himself, because he's the Captain and is meant to be responsible for safeguarding all of our lives, so he needs his space to meditate upon vital questions of strategy and logistics … or to make sweet love to the life-support officer, as it turns out.

Even Dimwit Donal can see I'm a bit upset. Worrying that I may have had designs on Harriet myself, he says nervously, "I know she's not your type, Fletch!"

"Put your mind at rest, I don't fancy her at all." This is

completely true. If I have admired Harriet's rear view it's only because it's such a contrast to her face. "I'm not jealous, you fecking dimwit. I'm wondering how we're going to hang onto the ship, since you've pissed Penelope off to the point that she's complaining about you to the backers!"

He cringes, and for a moment I feel sorry for the man.

"I taped over the camera in my cabin," he says weakly.

"*And* all the cameras in the corridors, so Penelope wouldn't see you and Harriet vanishing in there together?"

Another cringe.

"Whatever she hasn't seen, she'll be imagining worse," I say relentlessly.

At about this point you are probably wondering who Penelope is. We don't talk about her much, because the situation makes everyone uncomfortable.

But the fact is Penelope is our donor.

CHAPTER 7

Some spacers call their donors chain dogs, because that's what they do, they hook onto the Railroad. This use of jargon is a pathetic attempt to compensate for their own inferiority complexes. So we'll just go with *donor*. I don't have an inferiority complex. Do you?

Penelope is a donor, ergo she is a stacker. *This* technology we human beings developed all by our little selves, before the Railroad came along. Actually it's a collection of technologies and practices—nootropics, prep schools, chips implanted in your brain, assortative marriage, prebirth genetic screening—they *stack* all these things together, and the end result is they're so much smarter than the rest of us, they're basically a different species.

Some scientists say they've already diverged from the rest of us. They've got better genes.

So what do stackers do with their great brains?

The usual:

Manage hedge funds

Work as consultants

Get useless degrees in the humanities

Run governments

Reverse-engineer A-tech

Raise the next generation of stackers

And when they're bored of all that …

Operate spaceships

There are always more would-be donors than there are ships. Apparently, for a certain type of stacker, it's a huge thrill to be bedded down in the control room of a spaceship, communing on an intimate level with its computer systems, racing along the Interstellar Railroad, helplessly dependent on your Captain to deliver your daily whipping.

And they talk about it like it's this selfless volunteer activity.

Many stackers have a dirty secret, you see. They feel bad about their natural and unnatural advantages. They want to be kicked. Quite a lot of them literally want to wear uniforms and be ordered around on the end of a leash.

We had the bad luck to land one who likes to wear crotchless panties and be ordered around on the end of a leash, and if you think that sounds like fun, I can only assume you've not spent years holding the leash's other end, trying to think up ways to please her.

Because it's the donors who've got all the power. Of course it is. Spaceship operation is way over the heads of average joes like you and me. You've got to interface in real time with the AI subroutines and the Railroad's energy conversion algorithms and Jesus knows what. I had a go once; I felt like a monkey trying to type Shakespeare.

No stackee, no flyee.

So they get to travel the galaxy and use us to act out their psychosexual dramas at the same time. *Sweet!*

On the whole though, the donor system functions well, with a Darwinian hierarchy built in. Lots of stackers want to be donors, but do we want a gap-year kid with an IQ of 200 and itchy feet? No. What we want—what every crew wants—

is a *rich* donor ... one who can kick in for construction and maintenance.

Penelope Adele Saltzman fit the ticket perfectly. She'd had a high-flying career in public relations, made a lot of money one way and another, but her needs weren't being met.

She fell for Donal O'Leary's good looks and was charmed by his decision to name his ship *Skint Idjit,* once she'd had it explained to her. I can still see them in that bar in New York, Donal waxing lyrical— *"Skint,* you see it means broke, no money in the bank. And *idjit,* no it doesn't mean idiot, it's more affectionate ..." Myself ordering up another round of Guinness, thinking he was laying on the stage-Irish too thick and she'd laugh and walk away any minute now.

But she didn't.

So much the worse for her.

I glance down at the floor of the freezer; she's somewhere below us, in the control room, and I feel an urge to lower my voice even though I know there are no cameras or mics in the freezer. That would be why the Captain is hiding in here in the first place. "I know you aren't really into the BDSM shite," I say, "but can't you just go through the motions to keep her happy?"

The Captain has confessed he's been neglecting Penelope's needs, on top of betraying her (as she sees it) with Harriet.

He shakes his helmeted head. "I just can't do it anymore," he says, and I understand.

I understand.

I pat his armored shoulder. "Don't worry. Ruby can't have you fired for being a two-timing love rat."

"I know," he says dolefully. "That's why he's trying to kill me."

I still think he may be imagining this. It would make sense

for Goldman Sachs to protect their investment in the *Skint Idjit*. But how would killing Donal accomplish that? It would have the opposite effect, sure …

… unless they believe—as I believed myself—that Donal's lost it. That he no longer has what it takes.

I don't believe that anymore. What I see in front of me is a man who's just very distressed by the whole situation. He feels things more than I do, more than I allow myself.

That said, he's clearly had his last straw. We can't continue on like this.

Fortunately, we don't have to.

"We've just got to get back to Arcadia." I say. "Offload the A-tech and we'll be laughing all the way to the bank."

I throw open the door of the freezer. Suckass's heat feels like a hug.

Uznadze is sitting on one of the kitchen counters, shooting the breeze with one of Trigger's assistants. "Is anyone down at the flitters?" I demand.

I'm terrified that someone will find Morgan's body, which is still in the cargo pod of my flitter. They wouldn't even have to get very close, considering the smell of him.

"Oh sure, yeah, boss. Toroshelidze keep watch."

I have to get down there, I can't leave it any longer, but now here comes Saul to update us on the progress of the repairs. Harriet's with him. She brushes past me, straight into the freezer, and the lovelight is burning in her eyes. I must have been blind.

The repairs are finished, Saul says in his roundabout way. The Captain comes clanking out of the freezer, looking like a skinny snowman, his exoskeleton all coated with frost. "We leave for Arcadia at midnight, ship time," he announces.

And then he unzips his exoskeleton.

It crumples to the kitchen floor, a puddle of A-tech with an angular weld in the middle, and he steps forth like a great baby with hairy legs and stubble. "I'll just go and tell Penelope," he says, his voice wavering only a little. "Coming, Fletch?"

I can't. I have to go and dispose of Morgan's body.

But it's obvious the Captain needs moral support.

If I let him go by himself, he might end up giving in to her. Telling her about our find, just to keep her quiet, as he'd see it. And she'd tell GS. I know she talks to them regularly.

We've got no comms with Earth out here, unless we fire a message capsule into orbit and send it skidding along the Railroad all the way back to Arcadia. But once we're back on Arcadia, there's the interstellar postal service, only two days round-trip. She could blow the gaff on us before Sakashvili has a chance to arrange the auction. So Donal *has* to keep quiet.

Oh, feck. I'd better go with him. Toro-what's-his-name can stand guard for another few minutes.

"Sure, I'll come," I say, and we head down to the control deck, stopping off along the way for the Captain to put on some clothes.

CHAPTER 8

All control decks look like dungeons to me. You can paint ten thousand computers in cheery colors and stick vases of plastic flowers around the place, but it's still a cavern with ten thousand computers in it. Screens flash and blink, chimes go off, and AI voices say terrifying things such as "Turbine status: Manually shut down due to a boiler feed pump issue."

I generally try to forget that we live on top of a 2.3 gigawatt nuclear reactor.

Of course this stuff is mother's milk to Penelope. She's sprawled in her couch when we come in, making numbers dance.

The instant she sees the Captain, she rolls out of the couch and goes to her knees, head bowed, eyes downcast.

Penelope is 49, a few years older than us, but being a stacker, she doesn't look it. Her long slender limbs are milky pale, her baby-doll negligee skims taut cleavage, and her jawline is as fine as the blade of a knife. I can't help mentally comparing her with Harriet. Guess who loses.

"How may I serve you, Master?"

Penelope can talk like an ordinary person over the intercom, but put her face to face with Donal and it's 'Master' this, 'Master' that. I'm really not sure about those nootropic drugs they take. Penelope's whole personality seems like a side-effect.

"You may get up," the Captain says.

She stands up.

"You may fetch me a beverage."

"What kind of beverage, Master?"

"Ah, iced coffee. And one for Fletch."

Ah God no. I don't want to be drinking iced coffee, I want to transact our business and get out of here, but I know he's softening her up. I say, "I'll have mine hot."

I'm chilled enough already.

"He'll have his hot," the Captain repeats.

She moves gracefully to her little kitchenette. Miss Penelope doesn't eat and drink in the mess with us proles. "Would you like milk and sugar, Master?"

"Nah, just black."

"I'll have milk and sugar," I say.

"He'll have milk and sugar."

"One spoon or two?"

"Two," I say.

"Two," the Captain repeats.

"Yes, Master."

See what he has to go through? I'd choose Harriet, too, even if she has got a face like the back of a bus.

When Penelope has served our coffees, Donal just crashes it out. "Penelope, we will be returning to Arcadia at zero hundred hours, ship time."

She's standing in front of us in her 'servant' posture, head bowed, hands demurely folded. You can see her true age in those hands. I'm looking at them and so I see the knuckles whiten with shock at the Captain's announcement. No wonder. We were supposed to explore fifty planets down this spur, or until we found something, and as far as she knows we haven't.

But all she says is, "Yes, Master."

"Will you be able to get the ship ready for launch?"

"Yes, Master."

"If you need more time, let me know."

"Yes, Master."

"Is our propellant situation OK, then?"

"Local foraging has yielded sufficient propellant for an estimated four orbital round trips, Master."

By this she means that Saul's lads have been collecting rainwater and feeding it into the splitter, which gives us hydrogen for the engine.

"Very good," the Captain says. Seemingly at a loss, he shuffles his feet, takes a sip of the unwanted iced coffee, puts it down dangerously near a keyboard. I'm trying to telepathically beam at him that our mission is accomplished and we can get out of here now. "Well," he says.

The door hisses and Ruby peers around it. "Boy, this place is a mess," he says, eyes going wide.

Apart from the fact that he's not supposed to be in here, he does have a point. Plastic flowers and a cheery paint job are our contributions to the décor, but Penelope has also made her own contributions, e.g. dirty underwear dropped where she took it off, used mugs and crockery laid down wherever she finished with them, cuddly toys, souvenirs, and then there are the dildoes and restraints lying around.

Ruby ducks under the anti-grav bed, Penelope's little luxury. Not so little, actually. It's a king-size, currently hovering near the ceiling. I can't help cringing as he stops underneath it to pick up an energy bar wrapper.

"You can leave that, Ruby," the Captain says. He sticks his

jaw out. "What do you want?"

Ruby straightens up from under the bed. "What's this I hear about going back to Arcadia?"

"Ah yes," the Captain says. "You've heard correctly. We are returning to Arcadia."

He is shite at this. I wish I hadn't told him anything. The Butterfly-zillas could have stayed in the freezer until we explored fifty planets out, turned around, and came back, no one any the wiser.

"Why?" says Ruby, predictably. "There are dozens of worlds still out there to explore!"

Then the Captain surprises me. He roars at Ruby, "Because I've lost six of my men and women, that's why! I can't continue this exploration with only two scout groups! Unless *you'd* like to put together a scout group and lead it yourself, Mr. Ruby? Huh? Would you like to do that?"

Ruby physically flinches. "Uh, no. I don't think, um, I'm not cut out for scouting."

"And yet you were assigned to this ship as Deputy A-Tech Scout. Look at Fletch, he's not afraid to get out there and get his hands dirty when the need arises."

Leave me out of it, I think to myself. The whole point of being management is you get to do the easy bits and leave the dirty work to others. On the other hand, it hasn't really worked out like that recently.

Ruby shoots me a poisonous look, but decides that hypocrisy is the better part of valor. "Of course I'd be happy to field a new scout group, Captain, if that's what you think we should do. But can we spare the manpower from ship-crucial operations?"

"We cannot," the Captain says. "And that's why we're going back to Arcadia! Any more questions?"

Penelope twitches.

"Oh, for Christ's sake say what's on your mind, Penny!" the Captain snarls. "I mean, you have permission to speak."

That's all she needs. "I have no problem with the change of plan, Donal. You're the captain and I respect your decisions. But I do have a big fucking problem with your lies!"

Oh Christ, here it comes—

But of course, she doesn't know about any A-tech stashed in the freezer. She's barking up a different tree entirely. "We're going back to Arcadia so *you* can run off with that bridge-and-tunnel guidette!"

Harriet is an American just like Penelope. What's a bridge-and-tunnel guidette? Your guess is as good as mine.

"Penelope, if you're implying I would ever leave the *Skint Idjit,* you're very much mistaken," the Captain says coldly. "I *love* this ship. Didn't I build her with my own hands—"

"With my money!"

"If you want your investment back, you can have your investment back!"

Oh Christ, Donal, SHUT UP! He's thinking he could return Penelope's $1,500,000 investment in the *Skint Idjit* after we auction off the Butterfly-zillas. At the present time we don't have anything like that kind of money. She knows it and so does Ruby, whose eyes and ears are on stalks.

"I don't want my investment back," Penelope says, suddenly tearful. "All I want is to be treated the way I deserve."

I can see it is on the tip of the Captain's tongue to tell her to get stuffed. But …

… no stackee, no flyee.

And so he steels himself to play his role one last time. He steps towards Penelope, takes her by the hair, and swats her across the bottom. *"That's* what you deserve for speaking to me like that."

"Sorry, Master," cries Penelope.

"I'll make you sorry," the Captain says grimly, rolling up his sleeves.

Me and Ruby make a hasty exit. Out in the hatchway, at the foot of the ladder that leads up to the crew deck, our eyes meet. For the first time ever, we are of one mind. "Oh my God," Ruby says. "That is one hell of an unhealthy relationship."

"You're telling me." I gesture for him to go first up the ladder.

"If she's unhappy, why doesn't she just quit?"

"Maybe she will."

"I mean, she's a *volunteer*. She doesn't have to be here. I don't know why anyone volunteers for this shit."

"I think it's a mix of things," I say. "They see it as sticking up for the little guy, keeping the independents flying, so that the whole exploration industry doesn't fall into the claws of the investment banks."

But even independent ships like the *Skint Idjit* need funding, of which Jacob Ruby is physical proof. I give him a dirty look, and he blushes. "Activism is a form of narcissism," he mutters.

"Maybe, but in Penelope's case it was mostly that she fell for Donal."

And now that she knows he's cheating on her, maybe she *will* quit. That'd be the best of all worlds, really. I see the sense of what the Captain suggested, about repaying her investment as soon as *we've* been paid. All the same I can see my share getting smaller and smaller as the (still-theoretical) money gets spread out thinner and thinner. The Georgians, the Captain, and he'll want to share it with Harriet, and now

Penelope, who's next in line, the fecking ship's cat? Not that we have one—except for the treecats, which have already cost us a fortune in frozen meat, and Harriet will probably insist on keeping them if the money's there for it.

Well, I'll still have enough for a medium-sized planet, as long as the backers don't get wind of our discovery. And that means making sure Ruby stays blissfully ignorant.

"I think I'll go help Trigger with the supper," I say.

There will be a slap-up supper for our last night on Suckass, as is *Skint Idjit* tradition. Trigger will need to be getting things out of the freezer. I'll help him with that.

CHAPTER 9

T-01H55M and holding. I *finally* sneak away to bury Morgan.

Sakashvili is waiting impatiently by the flitters. "All right, you can go," I say. "Stay off the vodka. I need you to keep an eye on Ruby."

"That dumb American. Who care what he do?"

"If he finds the Butterfly-zillas, we're toast, idjit. Don't let him near the freezer. Radio me if he's acting suspiciously."

"Yeah, yeah." Sakashvili beetles off. He's pissed that he's been stuck out here while everyone else was eating and drinking and making merry.

I know I should have come earlier but it was a great atmosphere, everyone delighted to be leaving Suckass at last, dizzy with relief that the Captain seems to be back to his old self.

I don't know what went on in the control room after I left. The Captain looked a bit pale when he emerged, but a dram or two fixed that.

I check that the flitters hide me from the *Skint Idjit*. Then I heave Morgan out of my own flitter's cargo pod.

If you've never handled a corpse that's been lying for 36 hours in tropical heat, you'll find this hard to believe, but it's true: I lose my supper then and there.

He doesn't even look like Morgan anymore.

But he *is* Morgan and I am bloody well going to give him a decent burial. He should have had 1/3rd of a fortune. Instead he'll be getting six feet of Suckass. But it is all I can do for him now.

It seems to take me an hour to reach the treeline. We should have parked closer to the geraniums. Morgan was a big guy and he seems heavier dead than he ever was alive.

I lay him down under the geraniums and trot back to the flitter for my entrenching tool. My mouth tastes of puke. My shadow stretches before me.

On any ordinary planet I would have the option of doing this under cover of darkness, but on Suckass, as previously noted, it's always day. I feel conspicuous. Mercifully, there's no one in sight except for Sakashvili, attaching his flitter to the cargo winch. I have my radio on, and through the static I hear the skirling of a violin. Good old Captain! I suggested that he might get out his fiddle and give them a bit of a ceili, and it sounds like he's doing it.

I attach the entrenching tool to my belt so I can carry that and Morgan at the same time. Peeping out of the shade, I see a group of six flitters circling in to land.

Scout Group C—the South Africans—is back. That makes everyone. We could theoretically launch any time now.

Sure enough, Saul's voice crackles out of my radio: "Resuming countdown. T minus one hour fifty-five minutes."

Better get cracking.

I carry Morgan deeper into the geraniums. It is dim here, amidst the shifting dapples of reddish light. Twenty yards, thirty yards … I'm scared of losing my way. This'll just have to be good enough.

I dig.

It goes fast enough for the first foot or so, but then I hit the roots of the geraniums. These turn out to be as tough as steel. My entrenching tool has an axe edge and an electric saw edge. I start off with the saw edge but it takes too long to saw through each root. The axe works better. I stand with my legs apart, pull it straight back over my head, and swing it straight down. Lift. Swing. Lift. Swing. I feel like my dad, swinging an axe on our farm at home. Oh, he wasn't a farmer. No one farms in Ireland anymore, except for a few boutique dairy operations. But we had an old wooden boat and when it got beyond repair, Dad chopped it up for firewood. I remember being impressed at how smoothly and powerfully he swung the axe. When he finished, he said to me, "Well, I didn't do a bad job, did I? Maybe it's in the genes."

Maybe it is in the genes. And here I am, the great-grand-son of Irish potato farmers, digging a grave for my friend, 2.3 kiloparsecs from Earth. What happened?

The work is good. Soothing to my soul. I shovel the chopped-up roots and soil out of the hole. Another round of axe work, some more shovelling, and now I've got a vaguely rectangular grave about three feet deep. I'd like to go deeper but my arms are shaking, sweat's pouring off me, and I decide this'll do.

"Come on, Morgan, in you go." I tumble him into the hole.

Leaning on my entrenching tool, I feel like I should say something, but I don't know what, apart from sorry. Sorry you aren't coming with us, Morgan. When I get my planet, I'll name a continent after you.

"T minus forty-five minutes. Propellant level sensor checks complete," says Saul on the radio.

This can't be all. There has to be something more.

I fold my dirty hands in an attitude of prayer, and begin

haltingly: "In the name of our Lord, may his soul rest in peace, and, uh …"

"Idjit, that's not it."

The Captain's voice spins me around. He's stomping through the trees, wearing his party gear—Wranglers and a short-sleeved cowboy shirt with pearl buttons.

"You need to be on board for the countdown," I snap.

"I just want to say goodbye to him. I was the one that offered him the bloody job. He wouldn't have been here otherwise."

Donal is carrying his violin.

"Are you going to play that?"

"I thought about it."

"I can't remember a fecking thing about funerals."

"You'll remember this."

He sets his fiddle under his chin and bows a melody, and Jesus, I *do* remember it. When the first part comes back around, I join in, singing:

Now the green blade riseth, from the buried grain,
Wheat that in the dark earth many days has lain;
Love lives again, that with the dead has been:
Love is come again, like wheat that springeth green.

It's an Easter hymn, but that feels appropriate. Ireland became an irreligious country around the turn of the century. But lately the Church has been making a comeback. Not coincidentally, the revival dates to the years of panic and confusion after the arrival of the Railroad. When you're suddenly given a galaxy to explore, what do you do? You beat a path to the nearest church, that's what. And if you think that doesn't make sense, just wait until you've explored a few hundred planets in the mold of Suckass, and dirtied your hands picking through the rubble of a dozen alien civilizations, all of them dead. Wait until you've buried an old friend on an alien planet.

Donal's fiddle skirls plaintively through the geraniums and it's almost like we've made a church of the twilit halls beneath the leaves. I've seldom felt so far from home. Tears are dripping down Donal's face, and I'm on the point of choking up myself, until Ruby says, "Hey, I never knew you had such a good singing voice, Fletch."

Me and Donal spin around. I nearly stumble into the grave. Ruby walks closer.

"What're you doing?" he says in that me-so-clueless way of his.

We might still be able to bluff this out. "We're burying our friend," I say coldly.

"In secret. Half an hour before launch?"

"As you do," I say, and lunge for my entrenching tool.

Donal's shout stops me. "He's got a gun!"

He does. It is a Glock, nice and small and concealable, and he's aiming it at Donal's heart.

No more Mr. Nice Guy, I guess.

And I left my lightsaber on board.

Donal's hands automatically go up. His fiddle falls to the ground. He winces—that fiddle is an old companion—and Ruby chuckles coldly. "Don't worry, I'll bury it with you." He motions with the Glock. He's twenty feet from us. Too far to rush him. Close enough that he won't miss. "Get into that hole."

"It's not big enough for the three of us," Donal says.

"Yeah, Fletch is obviously better at singing than digging. Whatever. I just thought you'd prefer to be buried rather than left to rot on the ground."

I start to edge away from Donal, moonwalking half an inch at a time. We might have a chance if I can reach my entrenching tool. Come on, Donal, keep him talking!

"It's awfully dark," Donal says, looking up at the chinks of sky we can see through the geranium canopy.

He's right actually, it is dark, and I realize what *that* means half a second before the sky opens.

It's like God is emptying his bathtub up there.

Thank you, Suckass!

Ruby twitches as the first splatters hit his face. His aim drifts.

I fling myself on the entrenching tool.

The Glock barks.

Donal staggers, blood fountaining.

I scream and charge at Ruby. The recoil has knocked him off balance, and I'm on him before he can recover. I whirl the entrenching tool at his head. I don't connect. Not because he's quick but because he's slipped in the leaf muck. He goes down on one knee, and the Glock flies out of his hands.

Berserk with rage, I swing the entrenching tool at him like an axe. Maybe it's in the genes, as my dad said.

But Ruby's rolling sideways, slipping and sliding, on his feet and darting away. *His* ancestors must've been rabbits.

I snatch up the Glock. We used to carry these on the Draco Spur, in addition to our laser rifles and sawn-off shotguns and every goddamn tool for slaughter we could get hold of.

BLAM! BLAM! BLAM! BLAM! BLAM!

He's vanished among the geraniums. I can't tell if I've hit him or not. The rain is sheeting down—it's at that stage now where the water dripping off the leaves is a downpour in its own right.

The Glock is empty, the barrel so hot the rain sizzles on it. I throw it down and turn to Donal, dreading what I'll see.

"Help me up, you gobshite!"

"Jesus, you're alive!"

He looks old with pain. He's clutching his right arm. Blood wells between his fingers and runs down his arm, turning pink as it mixes with the rain. "I need to get a tourniquet on this."

"Right you are." I take off my t-shirt and knot it around his arm above the horrible gouge where the bullet tore through flesh and muscle. This slows the rate of blood loss, but he's fading on me, going into shock in front of my eyes. I get on the radio. "Harriet, Harriet, come in."

All I hear is my own ears ringing from the gunshots. I try the other channels. "Harriet, Saul, Woolly, where are you guys? Captain's down!"

Saul proclaims faintly, "T minus fourteen minutes and holding. Verify all systems ready for crew deck closeout."

Feck!

I pick the Captain up. I carried a dead friend out here and now I'm carrying a half-dead friend back. Sorry, Morgan, I don't have time to fill in your grave. I hope you understand.

At the end of my strength, I stagger out from the treeline into the sheeting rain.

The *Skint Idjit* glows like a sideways Christmas tree through the downpour. These clusters of pretty lights indicate that she is ready to launch. All the flitters have been stowed on the flight deck except the last one, which is presently rising in the cargo winch, and below it, on the ground, squats Ruby, waiting for the winch to come back down.

I am going to murder Sakashvili. He was supposed to keep an eye on this freak.

I drag Donal across bare earth speckled with geranium

shoots. Ruby doesn't look around until we're nearly on top of him. He's wounded. I *did* hit him. Unfortunately it doesn't seem to be very serious. He staggers upright, favoring his left leg.

I lay Donal carefully on the grass and take a swing at Ruby. He reels out of range. It's comical, actually. I'm so exhausted I can't even land a punch on a man with a bullet in his leg.

"Why," I gasp, "are you," gasp, "trying to kill us?"

"Got no beef with *you,* Fletch." He glances up hopefully. The winch is descending.

I take this opportunity to punch him in the gob. It hardly even qualifies as a punch, more of a tap, but he lets out a squawk that turns into a scream as he inadvertently puts his weight on his bad leg.

"What's your fecking problem?" I pant. "Donal says you've been trying to kill him ever since Arcadia."

Ruby yelps, "Goldman Sachs dispatched me to make sure Ms. Saltzman was OK. They were not happy with the situation on board, and I believe their concerns are valid!"

So Donal was right. This *is* about Penelope. "What are the backers concerned about, specifically?"

"Based on her reports, they think she could be suicidal."

"Jesus Christ, she's not suicidal, she's submissive. You know what that means?"

"Yes, I know what that means, and the two things are not mutually exclusive."

"She's a donor. Goldman Sachs doesn't understand donors," I sneer. Although most of the shitheads who work at GS are stackers themselves, they do not understand the donor mindset. They can't conceive of why a person, especially a stacker, would do anything without being paid for it. Actually I can't either, but I'm not the one with fifty million dollars tied up in the *Skint Idjit.*

"They understand donors fine," Ruby snaps."They understand that if a donor dies in the field, his or her ship is stuck until help arrives! Which could be *years*, way out here."

"We've got self-propelled message capsules. More like a week."

"All the same, time is money. They didn't want to take that risk, which is why I'm here. And I've determined that the primary risk to Penelope's mental health is *him.*"

A jerk of his chin at Donal.

Following his gaze, I see that the cargo winch is about to touch down on top of Donal. I yank his unresponsive body out of the way just in time.

The bucket hits the mud, splashing us.

Over the side of the bucket rises the grinning face of Sakashvili.

He is pointing a laser carbine at me.

I don't even curse him out. I am just too tired. It's myself I should be cursing, anyway, for trusting this pimply Georgian mafioso.

"Gimme a hand," Ruby says. Sakashvili ignores him. He is intent on covering me. Ruby hauls himself into the bucket with a grunt of pain. I wonder why Sakashvili is letting Ruby on board, instead of shooting him as would be more sensible. He probably thinks the backers would be more upset to lose Ruby than to lose Donal and me, and he is probably right.

I start to move towards the winch, and Sakashvili lays an energy pulse at my feet.

"Aw c'mon, let's take Fletch," says Ruby.

"No," Sakashvili says. "This fucker always make others do the hard work. Lazy fuck Irish. He wipe ass with safety regulations, and others suffer!" He is bawling at me now. "Morgan, Aisling, Daphne, Shane, Fergal, Eamon, ALL DEAD because of him! No, no, Ruby. Shooting is too good for this piece of shit."

And I can't say anything, because he's right. It was my job to keep them out of trouble. I failed.

The scoop begins to rise, and it might be the rain getting in Sakashvili's eyes, but I'm 99% certain he winks at me.

Meaning: *I will be thinking of you when I'm counting my billions on Arcadia.*

There is only one way I might possibly spoil his triumph. I start shouting as loudly as I can.

"Look in the freezer! Ruby! LOOK! IN THE! FREEZER! LOOK IN THE FREEZER RUBY IN THE FREEZER IN THE …"

The wind knocks the scoop against the *Skint Idjit's* side. It reaches the airlock, with no sign that Ruby has heard me.

The crane arm retracts into the airlock, taking the scoop with it.

The airlock closes.

Saul's imperturbable voice says on the radio, "Countdown resuming. T minus three minutes."

I look up at the humungous bulk of the *Idjit.* Then I look around the LZ, which we scorched to the raw earth with our engines when we landed. And then—I'll never know afterwards how I managed it—I hoist Donal onto my back and I start to run.

CHAPTER 10

Well, Fletch, you wanted a planet, you've got a planet.

And you even get to share it with your best friend.

It's a shame Donal is too poorly to appreciate our luck, but nothing's perfect.

"Just call me King Fletcher," I tell him, cracking a water purification capsule into a thermos full of rainwater.

If you're easily disgusted, you can skip this next bit. I went back to Morgan's body and fetched all the kit that was on him. Of course the battery-powered shite was dead, but that still yielded a haul of:

24 water purification tablets

5 ration bars

1 balisong knife

1 A-tech thermos

1 solar-powered emergency beacon

and 1 portable solar still (this last item is GOLD, we'd be dead already without it).

I did *not* encourage my people to ignore safety regulations. There's a middle ground between being reckless and being an 'elf 'n' safety nerd like Sakash*villain*, and Morgan had it dialed in, at least until that final risk he took, which killed him.

Well, we're likely enough to join him before long.

We've exactly one third of one ration bar left, and I have

had no luck hunting with my entrenchment tool.

There *are* animals on Suckass. The ones we know about look like large rats. They're extremely shy but I have spotted a few of them about since the *Skint Idjit* left. It's as if they know that very soon they'll have the planet to themselves again.

I support Donal's shoulders with one arm and tip the thermos to his lips, as if I'm feeding a baby. "Just imagine it's whiskey," I tell him.

"Very funny," he croaks. Some of the water goes into his mouth. More trickles into his stubble. "Sorry, sorry, man."

"Not to worry, there's more where that came from."

There are not a lot more water purification tablets, but we shouldn't need them anyway, having had A-tech immune shots. I'd just rather be safe than sorry. After all, *something* has caused Donal's arm to puff up like a football. The wound is red and inflamed. Pus weeps from the raw mouth of it. And the redness is spreading along his arm in both directions. I've never seen anything like this in real life, but some kind of ancestral memory tells me it is an infection. If it goes untreated much longer he will die.

It feels like a year since the *Skint Idjit* launched; in fact it's been five rains. That's about 70 hours. I resist the temptation to check the actual time. My radio's all I've got for a clock and I've turned it off to save the battery. I had a solar charger for it, but I fed that to the Butterfly-zillas last week.

On the day the *Skint Idjit* launched, I managed to haul Donal far enough away that we didn't get crisped, although I felt the heat of her lift-off burn on my back. We've now re-occupied our bivouac at the treeline. Some careless sod left a hammock behind, and I also found a torn groundsheet which I've rigged up in the lowest branches to keep the rain off us.

More and more often, I catch myself thinking about that abandoned campsite I found on my journey to the terminator. It seems more sinister to me now. I imagine some guy stuck on Suckass, abandoned by his shipmates like us, surviving for a little while … and then quietly creeping into the trees to die.

For it's a dead certainty, if you'll excuse the pun, that we can't survive on Suckass.

At least, not in this region of Suckass.

After Donal dies I will start walking east, towards the nearest river. There may be fish. The fish may be easier to catch than the rats, *if* I get there. It's almost a hundred miles, as I recall. I'm hungry already and you can't eat geranium leaves (tried; puked). When I'm in a real mood, I wish Donal would hurry up and die so I can be away.

Jesus have mercy.

Jesus have mercy.

The local loop of the Railroad taunts me. It says: I've got more ways to kill you than you ever imagined. You were worried about pirates, claim-jumpers, complex metazoans? I can kill you just by leaving you alone.

Such thoughts as these are running darkly through my mind when a star peels off the railroad and blazes out, brighter than Suckass's cool little sun.

That's a spaceship.

It has just disengaged from the Railroad on a deorbit trajectory.

I'm a heartbeat from running out into the clearing to shout and wave, like a loony.

"Donal! It's a ship! We're saved!"

He breathes stertorously, which is all he's done for the last twelve hours or so.

The star shoots across the sky and vanishes behind the curve of the planet. Feck, *feck!* They're going to land thousands of miles from us!

I turn on my radio. It's got one bar of battery power left but it's not got a very great range. Turn it off again.

And then I remember about the other thing I found on Morgan's body.

His solar-powered emergency beacon.

I carry it into the sunlight, set it up, and turn it on to broadcast at maximum power.

I'm so excited, I forget my hunger.

I remember it again fairly soon, as the leaves rustle in the wind and Donal moans in his fevered sleep and nothing else happens.

Maybe I imagined that ship.

Maybe I was hallucinating.

Clouds roll out of the west and it starts to rain.

The rain has just about cleared up when three flitters soar over the geraniums and glide into the clearing.

These flitters are black, with charging elephants haloed in flames painted on their pods. This is bad news. It's unbelievably bad news. But I'm so relieved to see them that I run out heedlessly to meet them as they bounce to a stop in the sticky mud. "Hello! Hello there! We need help!"

The pilot of the lead flitter hops out. He responds in the universal jargon of the exploration industry, by pointing a weapon at me.

This weapon is a lightsaber, the twin of my own.

"Stay right where you are," he growls.

It's my uncle Finian.

He's well over seventy, clad in black from head to toe, with a belt buckle in the shape of an elephant. An Old Testament beard cascades over his substantial belly.

Has he come all this way to kill me? I wouldn't put it past him.

"Are you going to shoot me, Uncle Finian? Make up your mind," I say.

CHAPTER 11

My uncle Finian, my dad's big brother, was a surface rat in the days when there *were* surface rats, before we found the A-tech immune booster stuff. Him and his mates would EVA in spacesuits on alien planets with perfectly good atmospheres, looking like 20th-century astronauts, searching for A-tech with robot sniffer dogs. It was easy to get a job on the Railroad in those days. You just had to be insane, suicidal, or willing to risk your life to play the A-tech lottery.

Finian was all three, according to my parents. That only encouraged me to worship him and wish with all my childish heart that I could be *just like him* one day.

I joined Finian's crew the day I turned eighteen. He had his own ship by then. We operated on the Draco Spur, picking up pennies ahead of the lumbering corporate fleets. This was before Wall Street got clever with their outsourcing strategies. There were planets out there for the claiming and in retrospect, I should have claimed one for myself, but I was having too much fun and what I ended up claiming for myself was that lightsaber.

I stuffed it into my suitcase and took it back with me to Lisdoonvarna.

I was showing off with it in the beer garden behind O'Donoghue's pub when in walks Finian and decks me. It turns out he was planning to register the beam mechanism as a new discovery, and by taking the thing back to Earth and waving it around in public, I'd established prior art. So there went millions of dollars for Finian, and there went my job.

By that time Donal had trudged through his spaceship engineering course and got all the licenses and cleared the regulatory hurdles they make you jump before you can get your own ship. So I had a way back into the business. Finian gave us a hand at times, as Donal's father is a big man in the nuclear industry and that's a connection you want to have, but he always made it clear he wasn't doing it for me.

He's a legend in certain circles. Did you know there are pirate fan clubs? There are and all. These wee idiot boys on Earth subscribe to his updates and he sends them elephant pins and t-shirts and shite. They probably want to be *just like him* when they grow up.

His ship is called the *Marauding Elephant,* of course, and when we arrive on board, after a long, bumpy flitter trip, I struggle not to laugh. He's made a lot of improvements since I was last on board. The interior of his up-armored Airbus A990 is now tarted up like the Playboy mansion, with a jacuzzi and 100-inch tellies, oldies blasting from the sound system and solid gold elephants on every bloody thing.

The crew's combined ages run into the high four figures. They're Finian's mates from his surface rat days, which is to say they all come from West Clare. Now they're living the life of kings. Nepotism's a wonderful thing.

But it only goes so far, and Finian makes it clear that blood's not thicker than water when he marches me into the bogs and slams me against the wall. There are gold elephants embossed on the tiles. A sharp edge opens my scalp. "Ow feck!"

"Where's the fucking A-tech?" Finian growls.

He's got his lightsaber jammed under my jaw. One ounce of pressure from his thumb and it'll stab through my brain.

I try to speak without moving my jaw. "It's on the nightside. Go and get it yourself if you've the bollocks for it."

"Fuck off, cunt. There was a beacon, as arranged, we go to retrieve the stuff, and there's nothing but yourself and Liam O'Leary's boy running a fever of a hundred and three. This is not satisfactory."

This is not satisfactory always was one of Finian's favorite phrases, usually to be followed by a severe kicking for the unfortunate crewman who'd prompted it. But now it's a different phrase that snags in my panicked brain: *As arranged.*

As arranged by who?

As arranged by Finian and Donal, of course, and if Donal wasn't in the *Elephant's* sickbay right now with an IV in his arm and the entire ship's supply of antibiotics in his blood, I'd murder him.

They must have planned it all out beforehand.

There we were on Arcadia, outfitting the *Skint Idjit* for an expedition along an unexplored spur of the Railroad. Goldman Sachs has claimed this whole spur, and funded our trip. Anything we find, 50% of it is theirs.

Unless we leave it where it is, and Finian comes along and picks it up later. Then him and Donal split the profit.

That's how they must have *arranged* it.

And Finian thinks I know about this cunning little scheme, but this is the first I've heard of it, because Donal never said a word. He was planning to cut me and Morgan out, so he could keep his whole share to set up with Harriet in a love-nest on Treetop, or maybe buy a floating island on Seventh Heaven, or some other clichéd yuppie thing.

No wonder he didn't seem too happy when I carted those body bags full of A-tech into the *Skint Idjit's* freezer.

Blood tickles the back of my neck, running down from the cut on my scalp. I swallow. The muzzle of the lightsaber grinds against my adam's apple. I grit out, "Put that away and I'll tell you how to get the A-tech."

He lowers his lightsaber a few inches. "I remember you stole one of these from me," he says broodingly. "They never were able to reverse-engineer the beam mechanism, did you know? There are only five or six in the universe, and they're each worth millions."

Finian Connolly, ladies and gentlemen. Grudges give him something to wake up for in the morning.

"I've still got mine," I say. "It's on the *Skint Idjit.*"

"Yeah, and where's that?"

"Probably about five hundred lightyears away. Is the *Elephant* still as fast as she used to be? We might be able to catch them."

"And tell me why I'd want to do that, when the A-tech is here, according to you."

"Because there are also samples on the *Idjit!* And if they get back to Arcadia first, it all belongs to Goldman Sachs." Or rather, to Lukas Sakashvili, after he murders Ruby as he ought.

"How did there get to be samples on the *Idjit?* You were supposed to leave them in situ for us to pick up."

I don't want to tell him Donal neglected to inform me about that part. I don't want him to think I'm gullible, even though I obviously am. So let him think I'm holding out on him. Let him think I might have more to give. "We've got a corporate spy on board," I say, which is after all true.

Finian scowls and runs his thumb over the pushbutton of

his lightsaber. The music from the lounge hits a sludgy cre-
scendo. I'm trembling, trying to hide it. One of the auld fellas
walks in and unzips at a urinal without so much as a double-
take. They've seen Finian kill in cold blood before, and will
not be surprised if they see it again. It makes no difference at
all that I'm his own brother's son.

"You were nothing but trouble when you worked for me,"
he says at last. "Always looking for the easy score. Dragging
the other lads into your crap wee schemes. Disobeying orders.
Thinking you could get away with murder because you were
my nephew."

He slots the lightsaber smartly into the holster on his belt,
which of course has a gold elephant on it.

"We'll see if you've learned your lesson."

I nod humbly.

It's true I learned a lot of things working for Finian. And
one of them is that honesty doesn't pay.

CHAPTER 12

So I get a temporary extension of my lease on life, which is my definition of a successful negotiation at this point.

And the *Marauding Elephant* charges out along the Interstellar Railroad.

The *Elephant* does not have a donor, per se. Finian is way beyond such conventionalities. He's instead procured himself a stacker of a very rare type: a rebel. This individual is called Milton Khan and he bends my ear about the moral turpitude (his words) of The Establishment. What does he think of Finian then? I dare not ask in case it induces cognitive dissonance.

"You want to keep an eye on that one," I tell my uncle. "One day he'll wake up and realize that he could be working for Wall Street, and you won't see him for dust."

"Were you having trouble with your donor on the *Idjit?*"

"A bit, yeah."

"You need to have a backup." He nods at one of the auld fellas, who raises his pint to us. "He's our backup. He worked in the City for forty years, then he decided to do something else with his life."

It's queer to see an old stacker. They usually hide away in think tanks and executive boardrooms. It's even queerer to see a stacker who doesn't *look* like one, and Milton Khan makes two. He wears purple spandex bike shorts. The ex-City geezer dresses like the rest of Finian's crew—leather jeans, rock 'n' roll t-shirts, pointy boots. It's as if they think they're living in *Mad Max,* the remake.

"Have you been back to Lisdoonvarna recently?" Finian asks me, boots on the bar, sipping Laphroaig.

"Not for a couple of years. Have you?"

I know he hasn't. My dad wouldn't let him into the house if he dared to show his nose. There are some in town who might even call the guards. It's a respectable community.

My thoughts probably show on my face. Finian scowls. "What are they saying about me these days?"

"Oh, the usual. But that's nothing to what they'll say if we lose the *Skint Idjit."*

"Don't you worry. The *Elephant's* capable of twice that old tub's top speed. We'll catch up to her … and the A-tech."

An hour or so later we sweep into the star system of Planet No. 27, the one we didn't bother to name because it is in pieces. The gandy dancers have not yet finished repairing the hole in the Railroad, but they have put up a detour that goes around it, closing the local loop.

As we race around the loop, Milton Khan lets out a cry.

I forgot to mention that Khan does not lurk in his own messy computer-filled lair like most of the donors I've known. On the *Elephant,* the control room is the bridge is the lounge, and Khan does his stuff on two laptops with a pair of noise-canceling headphones.

In one corner the auld fellas are watching Ireland v. Russia in the 2066 World Cup, and in this corner Khan is pointing at another of the big screens, which now shows the rubble of Planet No. 27.

"That's a ship!" he screeches.

"Slow down," I shout.

We are whipping around the local loop at a few percent of the speed of light. You can't feel it on account of the Railroad's gravity field, but Padraig, my uncle's pilot, is leaning into the curve like a motorcycle racer, the yoke slewed all the way over. "The feck I'm slowing down," he grunts.

Khan zooms in on the image he's captured. It is a blended-wing Boeing X-80. It is wedged into a crevice on a smallish fragment of Planet No. 27, near the center of the 100,000-mile-wide rubble cloud.

Honestly, the obituaries write themselves with our lot.

"That's the *Idjit,*" I howl.

"Is it now?" Finian purrs. "Go around for another pass, Paddy."

Around the loop we go again. This time Khan gets a better angle for the cameras. The *Skint Idjit* is unmistakably, indubitably stuck.

"The luck of the Irish strikes again," my uncle says happily.

"We have to go and get the A-tech off them," I say. But of course I am not thinking about the bleeding Butterfly-zillas. I am thinking about Harriet and Woolly and Saul and Saul's scruffy assistants and Trigger the cook and *his* assistants, and the South Africans and yes, even the Georgians. Not even a bastard like Sakashvili deserves to die of hunger and thirst. I should know. I've tried it.

Finian is indifferent. "We'll go back to Planet Geranium and get it there. *If* you've got the balls for it, Fletcher."

"Take us into the system, Khan," I say, chancing my arm.

"Boss?" says Khan.

"I'm not taking my baby into that shambles," Finian says. "Not on your fecking life."

"Harriet," moos a voice from the other end of the lounge. Jesus, it's Donal. On his feet, looking like a zombie fresh out of the grave. He's transfixed by the giant image of the *Skint Idjit* on the big screen. "Harriet!" he lows again.

"Away with you to bed," Finian says curtly.

I pivot back to the screens. We are coming up on the detour again. It just looks like a little bulge in the loop, and Finian's crew probably don't know why it's like that, because they never mentioned a hole in the Railroad, so it must have happened *after* they passed through …

"Oh, look," I say. "The track's dodgy up here," and I throw myself on Padraig, knocking him off the pilot's couch. Roars of fear and fury arise. Finian leaps at me.

I elbow him in the gut, grab the yoke, and steer the *Marauding Elephant* past the detour.

We sail straight off the broken end of the track and decelerate into the orbital space of Planet No.27.

Everyone sits down suddenly as we experience a split second of crushing gee-force before the inertial dampeners kick in. These are the same anti-grav A-tech that's in the flitters, amped up to compensate for the extreme deceleration you experience when coming off the Railroad.

Khan, moaning, engages the nuclear thermal drive. We backthrust into the rubble cloud.

When ten septillion tons of ex-planet are floating around in an area 100,000 miles across, the pieces are actually quite close together. It's like that bit in *Star Wars* where they fly through the asteroid belt, except real.

Last time I did this, I was trying to stay out of the rubble cloud. Now I'm flying into it. I jink and swerve, dodging potential impactors in three dimensions. The auld fellas hide under the furniture. Khan throws up. But he manages not to puke on his computers, and like a good stacker he holds it together, finessing our deceleration so that we land neatly on the shard where the *Skint Idjit* is wedged.

My heart is going like the clappers. My armpits are soaked with sweat. I can't believe I pulled that off.

Limp, I roll off the couch and confront my uncle. He's the only person still on his feet. Arms folded, he scowls for a second and then cracks a grudging smile. "At least you didn't kill us." The smile vanishes. "Now go and get a spacesuit."

I've only spacewalked a few times in my life. By the time I came along it was all shirtsleeves, and if the ship needs repairs in deep space, leave it to the propulsion guys. Finian lends me an EVA suit that must date back to his surface rat days. It's hot, constricting, and makes me look like a marshmallow with vestigial limbs.

We line up in the hall on this side of the airlock, armed to the teeth.

It's me, Finian, and a dozen of the auld fellas.

They aren't wearing marshmallows. They have custom spacesuits in the *Elephant's* colors of black and fiery red, with tusks on their helmets, honest to God, and bandoliers hanging off them and metalforma blades strapped to their thighs, and a blunderbuss for each one the size of a frigging saxophone.

Aren't the bloodyminded old feckers *ever* going to pack it in?

"Men!" says Finian, swinging his elephant helmet in one hand. "We are about to acquire a truly fecking stupendous prize, if my nephew is telling the truth! If he is not, I'll personally take responsibilty for gutting him. But be that as it may. That ship is defended only by a handful of explorers, who may well be dead by now anyway."

I raise my hand. "If you come across a pimply Georgian mafioso named Sakashvili, he's mine. Same goes for a Yank called Ruby."

"Very good," says Finian. "Apart from that, keep the carnage to a minimum, bearing in mind these are Donal O'Leary's guys. Old Elephants ... let's MARAUD!"

The auld fellas cheer, and we crowd into the airlock.

Spacewalking is not a game for the faint of heart.

I'm tumbling here and there over the rocky plain of sheared-off crust, feeling spacesick, because I'm not used to freefall. The inertial dampeners on our ships provide about half of Earth's gravity, even when you're not on the Railroad, and believe me, the difference between 0.5 gees and zero-gee is the difference between feeling fine and being sick in your mouth because you don't know which way is up and which way is down anymore.

I frantically pump my cold gas thrusters. The Old Elephants buzz ahead of me, belching fire from the much more powerful thrusters of these little space toboggans they've got. It is obvious that they will reach the *Skint Idjit* before I do, and I'm afraid they'll blow every living soul to pieces, regardless of Finian's mild suggestion to keep the carnage to a minimum. Carnage is what the Old Elephants *do.*

'Up' in the abyss of space, ginormous bergs of rock glint in the light of Planet No. 27's sun. That one looks like it's going to come 'down' and crush us. It's an illusion. It's thousands of miles away. I am spinning. I glimpse the *Skint Idjit's* nose, poking out of the crevice where she's wedged, and then the *Marauding Elephant* behind me, and then ...

What the feck is *that?*

"Ship!" I screech, praying my radio's working. "Finian! There's some fecker coming!"

"What?!?"

I can only gibber "ship, ship, ship." *Ship* is actually too kind a word for this monstrosity. It is the size of the *Skint Idjit* and the *Marauding Elephant* put together, a gigantic iron arrowhead with six thrusters. And it's got bloody huge broadside batteries and these have just laid down a stream of laser pulses on the *Marauding Elephant's* nose, ablating a few tons of the Airbus's shielding. This is what we in the business call a 'warning shot.'

The twelve-year-old trainspotter in me says "Lockheed-Martin F-99." But it can't be the USAF, because they wisely never leave our solar system. So it's military surplus, which means ...

"Pirates!" bellows Finian. "It's a trap! Back to the *Elephant*, boys!"

"This is the *Hellraiser,*" says a voice.

See? What did I tell you? *What did I tell you?* Everyone and his cousin thinks this is an acceptable way to make a living.

"Surrender immediately and you will not be harmed. Otherwise we will blow you to crap."

But the *Hellraisers* of the galaxy have never met my uncle.

"The feck you will," Finian booms.

And the *Elephant* is already lifting into space, corkscrewing like a spinning top, using her superior agility to dart out of the *Hellraiser's* field of fire, and now she comes out of her controlled tumble right on top of the larger ship. Feck, that Padraig is good. The *Elephant's* chain dogs glom onto the *Hellraiser* in a shower of electrical shorts. Trust them to find a violent use for the most innocuous technology. They're grappled!

The auld fellas scream past me, howling war cries and

hurling supersonic missiles at the *Hellraiser* from their toboggans, which turn out to have integrated railguns.

I do not have a toboggan, a railgun, *or* a death wish. I putter on as fast as my weak little thrusters will go, and dive into the *Idjit's* crevasse while the Old Elephants engage the *Hellraiser* from every point of the compass. I drift down between the sheared silicate cliff and the ironclad side of the *Idjit*. It's nice and dark down here. From a survivability point of view, this is definitely the best place to be right now.

A black butterfly flutters up to me, bobbing in the light of my helmet lamp.

Or, maybe not.

If that's one of our Butterfly-zillas, it's shrunk. It's only the size of my head.

"Feck off, you bastard!"

How did it get out of the ship?

I learn the answer to that when I reach the crew airlock. Three of the body bags are floating in the crevasse, bumping against the sides of the ship. Two of them are still lumpy. The other one's hooked on a razor-edged crag, which must have torn it open when it was thrown out of the airlock.

Butterflies converge on me. They clearly like the look of the powerpack on my EVA suit. I flail my arms at them. How did one Butterfly-zilla turn into hundreds of them?

Obvious answer: It had babies.

It must have felt in a cheerful reproductive sort of mood after all those tasty gadgets we fed it.

Fuzzy wings beat around my helmet. There's no air out here, so what are they flying in? The dark energy matrix or the fabric of spacetime itself or something. These are *not* animals, after all. They're A-tech. Ah Jesus, I'm fecked.

I slap wildly at the airlock's control pad. I can't see for butterflies. The green light goes on, I throw the hatch up and dive into the chamber, and about twenty buttlerflies get in with me and I have to spend the next quarter hour swatting them before I dare to cycle the airlock. They're nippy for their size but *if* you can catch them, you can kill them by smearing them on the walls. It must break their energy receptors or something. I don't *know*, Jesus, I'm guessing here! During the process my suit's powerpack dies. My air supply cuts out.

Lightheaded from breathing carbon dioxide, I fall out of the other end of the airlock.

I might as well not have bothered killing the butterflies in the chamber, because the ship is full of them.

A dense black cloud of them swarms me and then rises off, disappointed that I've no more easily accessible energy for them to suck.

Except for the energy that's in my own body, of course. So I can't take my helmet off. But I'll die if I can't breathe. I chin-press the toggle to raise my visor—good thing it's mechanically controlled. I press the toggle again immediately, leaving a half-inch slit to breathe through.

The butterflies swarm the slit. I'm wearing a beard of fuzzy wings that I have to keep plucking off with my gloves as I look around.

This is where we keep the EVA suits and the hull repair kit. All the EVA suits are still here.

And of course my radio's dead.

I shout, "Harriet! Saul! Woolly!" I even call Ruby's name, but the only answer I get is a familiar voice from behind me.

"Holy Mary, what a shambles."

"Donal!" He's squeezing out of the airlock in a marshmallow suit like my own, fending off butterflies with both hands.

"What're you doing here? You should be in bed."

"I'm not letting *you* rescue Harriet," he says.

"Rest your mind, I'm here to kill Sakashvili and Ruby, in whatever order I find them."

"You're just like your uncle, aren't you? Never let go of a grudge."

The criticism cuts unexpectedly deep, and I squirm for a moment, before remembering that this arsehole was going to cut me out of our big payday. "Yeah, Dimwit Donal," I say. "You're not so dim after all, are you? You were cute enough to arrange with Finian to split the proceeds, and me and Morgan none the wiser. That's a nice way to treat your oldest friend."

"Oldest friend," he says with a bitter laugh. "You'd have done the same to me if you got the ghost of a chance."

"I would not!"

I would have, actually.

"And I don't want any lectures from you about friendship!" He's properly pissed. This must have been building up for a while. "We put years of hard work into the *Idjit,* but that obviously means nothing to you. What do you care about all the blood and sweat and tears, what do you care about sticking together through thick and thin, good times and bad? All you want is your own planet, and everyone else can get stuffed. You've been halfway out the door for a long time."

He is right. I admit it, he is right. He may have a brain full of sentimental cliches but that doesn't mean he's wrong. I *was* on the edge of dumping the *Idjit* and buggering off to pastures greener … just like my uncle Finian.

But I refuse to let Donal grab the moral high ground like this. "If I've been a bit fecked off recently, I'm looking at the reason why! You've been lying down on the job for ages. My

God, sneaking around with Harriet, treating Penelope like a potted plant, you've not been here mentally or physically, and guess who's been doing your job for you?" I am yelling at him in genuine fury now. "I've been carrying you for six months, Donal, and I am fecking sick of it! You bet your arse I'll be dumping this lousy rotten tub … as soon as …"

I trail off lamely. We both look around through our cracked-ajar visors at the black puffballs roosting on the shelves. This lousy rotten tub is now nothing but a butterfly jar.

"I saved your life on Suckass, too, don't forget about that," I add.

Donal laughs hollowly. "Congratulations might be a wee bit premature," he says.

"The antibiotics worked, didn't they?"

"Not antibiotics. Anti*technotics*. Those bullets of Ruby's were softnoses with metalforma centers."

"Don't forget, he's mine," I say.

There is a pause and I hear the unspoken words: *if he's still alive. If anyone is.*

"All the EVA suits are still here," I observe.

"There should have been enough for everyone," Donal says.

But there weren't, because they broke down over the years and Donal never bothered to replace them. Cutting costs. So there were actually only eight. I don't remind him of this out loud. It would be gratuitously cruel.

"I guess we should split up," he says wearily. "I'll check the bridge. You check the crew quarters and the control room."

He's still avoiding Penelope, or maybe avoiding a sight of her corpse.

He pulls the laser carbine he's brought from the *Elephant*

around on its strap.

Of course, it is a dead hunk of metal, because the butterflies have drained its powerpack.

So is mine.

Well, it might come in handy as a club.

CHAPTER 13

I sidle through the corridors I know so well, holding my carbine by the stock. The reek of musty fur coats my nostrils. In reality this is probably the smell of muons being spontaneously disassembled or something of that nature. Six or seven butterflies crowd the bottom of my visor, trying to fit the points of their wings in through my breathing slit. I keep taking one hand off the carbine to wipe them away.

I am just doing this when someone jumps out at me from the Life Support office. I swing my carbine at them, one-handed, and connect with their torso. It doesn't have much effect because they are wearing an EVA suit with built-in body armor and an all-too-familiar logo on the chest: GOLD-MAN SACHS.

"You did this," I snarl, reversing my grip on the carbine.

Ruby's injured leg is obviously still giving him trouble. He lost his balance when I hit him and is trying to recover. I take a wide-legged stance and raise the carbine straight over my head.

"Wait! Wait! Fletch?!?"

"You let them out of the freezer." I swing the carbine straight down at his helmet.

He dodges, but not fast enough. The carbine chops into his visor, cracking it. The butterflies dancing around us dart at the crack. Unfortunately it's not big enough for them to fit in. As Ruby bats them away, I see that his visor is already webbed with cracks. He must have done that on purpose, to be able to breathe after his suit's air supply died.

"You told me to look in the freezer," he yells.

So he *did* hear me.

Feck, feck, feck.

That means I can't blame it all on him. It's my fault, too.

"I didn't tell you to go opening the body bags!" I shout.

"Sakashvili wouldn't tell me what was in them!"

"Is that little turd still alive?"

"I don't know. Let's find out."

We proceed to the crew deck. I keep Ruby ahead of me, although he keeps complaining he can't see through his cracked visor.

Whacking on closed doors, we confirm that the six South Africans are alive, stuck in their cabin, safe for now, although they've had to swat a lot of butterflies squeezing in through the ventilation ducts. One of them, Hendrik, got bitten and is in a bad way.

"As I thought," I say. "The Baby-zillas are more dangerous than the butterflies in the twilight zone. Those must have been the prototypes or something."

"Huh?"

"Oh, who the feck knows? It's A-tech. The point is with these ones, even the little guys can kill you."

"I think I've figured that out, thanks." Ruby's voice is dry. He tells me that when he stupidly opened the first body bag, hundreds of Baby-zillas poured out, and they killed Trigger and Trigger's two assistants on the spot.

Our cheerful cook, who could make the most delectable

frozen meals taste like mushy cabbage. He'll never break another microwave. I grit my teeth. "Why didn't they kill *you?*"

"I was wearing a biohazard suit," he says. "I'm not stupid."

"No, you're not are you, Mr. Wall Street?"

"I don't work for them anymore," he says.

"Good for you."

"They're not paying me enough for this." He swats at Baby-zillas with the energy of hysteria.

"If you're going to have a nervous breakdown, do it later."

"Oh, I already did that," he says. "Around about the time the Baby-zillas—that's a cute name for them, by the way—got into the bridge and killed Woolly, and we went off the Railroad. Or no, maybe it was when Saul successfully piloted us through this shit, only to get the ship stuck in a piece of a smashed planet. But all hope is not lost."

I am still hearing echoes of *killed Woolly*. Ruby said that like it doesn't matter, because it doesn't matter to him. All that matters to him is Jacob Ruby's wants and needs. "Woolly's dead! Is Saul dead, too?" I demand.

"Yeah, I'm pretty sure," he says. "One of his assistants, what's-her-name, might be on the reactor deck. The Baby-zillas can't have got in there yet, or we'd be suffocating in the dark."

I have never been able to remember the names of Saul's assistants either, which doesn't make me feel any better. "Is *everyone* dead?" Apart from the South Africans. That crew could survive a nuclear apocalypse.

"I'm pretty sure, yeah, they're all dead. Come on!"

"We've not checked the mess yet."

"That's where it started, man. Everyone's dead."

"What about Penelope?"

"We don't need her!" He's walking backwards, and now he

blocks my way, pleading, "We gotta get out of here!" He jerks on the strap of his rucksack. "I got spare powerpacks in here. This rucksack's A-tech, the Baby-zillas can't drain 'em. So we'll switch out the powerpacks outside—"

"You can't go outside with a cracked visor."

"Duct tape," he snaps, and then gets confidential. "I guess you've been hiding in the cargo hold, huh? Nice work sneaking in there." So that is where he thinks I sprang from. I was wondering. "You're the man, Fletch. You piloted us back onto the Railroad before. You can do any job you turn your hand to. I respect you more than anyone else in this crew ..."

Flattery from this one counts for less than nothing. Anyway, I'm no longer listening to him. From up ahead comes the sound of furniture falling over, or being knocked over.

I shove past Ruby and start to run—as much as you can run in a marshmallow.

Bursting into the mess, I smell smoke.

It's billowing from the kitchen. Someone must have used the broken microwave again. But that's not the worst news.

Half a dozen bodies in fluorescent yellow biohazard suits litter the floor, among overturned chairs and tables.

One person in a biohazard suit is still upright, stabbing with a mop at—

—a Rorschach blot that heaves and surges like living jelly—

—a dark matter eruption—

—one of the original Butterfly-zillas, it must be, except it's grown to ten times the size. It takes up half the mess. It now has so many wings that it's easy to see they aren't wings at all, they're rips in spacetime or partially unfurled hidden dimensions or something else you can't look straight at without hurting your eyes.

I wanted dragons. I got Cthulhu in drag.

And Sakashvili (his nametag's on his biohazard suit) is fighting it with a mop, using the handle like a spear, quite expertly it has to be said.

I recall that he once mentioned he enjoys medieval reenactments. That's what he wanted out of life, adventure with the full suite of health and safety regulations. That's why he went into the exploration industry. Not for this.

I know I've been talking about murdering him, but now that it comes down to it, murdering Butterfly-zilla seems much more important.

"Hey! Big and ugly! Over here!"

CHAPTER 14

"Nyah nyah nyah nyah!" I throw my carbine at Butterfly-zilla. It bounces off and hits the floor. It also distracts Sakashvili. Butterfly-zilla almost gets him. He recovers, shoves the mop into its maw, hurls himself towards me, and I take a couple of running steps into the mess, leaving him room to get out the door. Then I do the stupidest thing ever: I raise my visor another inch.

Butterfly-zilla reaches for me with pointed wings of darkness.

I toggle my visor down again and roll inelegantly out of the mess. Sakashvili drags me out and kicks the door shut.

"Will that hold it?" I shout, voice raw. I'm readjusting my visor so I can breathe.

"Fletch? How the fuck you get here?"

"Is this door going to hold it??"

"You save my life." Sakashvili sounds like he's crying inside his biohazard suit. "Shit fuck damn thing get everyone."

"All your lads. I'm sorry about that, Lukas." We are sprawling in the corridor amidst the usual cloud of Baby-zillas. These no longer seem so scary now I've met their mum. As soon as I catch my breath I get up and run. Sakashvili follows.

"You know why I fight it with the mop? Is *anti-grav* mop, for doing the ceilings." Slithering after me, he giggles tearfully.

"So?"

"Butterfly-zilla don't like anti-grav! I remember we kill the first one with the flitter. He get in the engine and die. No moving parts in flitter engine. Why he died? Anti-grav! This one bigger. With mop I hurt him. But not enough." He's giggling and snuffling again. "Wish I got anti-grav dolly, for to use like shield."

I skid to a halt. "Anti-grav! Fight A-tech with A-tech. That makes sense." Although what I'm really saying is 'fight a mystery with another mystery.' This inherit-the-stars business turns out to mean a whole lot of pushing buttons in the dark, and hoping to feck they aren't connected to things that go boom.

"The Captain's somewhere on the bridge deck." I talk over Sakashvili's astonishment. "Find him, and tell him what you just told me, and collect all the anti-grav gadgets you can find. I'm going to collect the EVA suits and take them to the South Africans." There will be enough for everyone, now that half of everyone is dead.

We split up and I go in search of Ruby.

I justify this to myself as going to check on Penelope.

Surprise, surprise, I find Ruby outside the door of the control room. "She won't let me in," he says in frustration.

"Yeah, but we don't need her anyway, do we?"

"What do you mean?"

"Why don't you tell me what you've got in mind, Ruby?"

He leans his helmet closer to mine. I can see the whites of his eyes between the cracks in his visor. "You probably haven't been outside, but there's a ship out there."

I feign surprise.

"It's called the *Hellraiser* or some damn thing. I EVA'd when we first got here. Made contact with them on the radio.

They've been here for months …"

I don't try to hide my astonishment. But I'm not astonished for the reason he thinks. The truth has finally dawned. That overgrown LZ I found on my way to the terminator? It wasn't made by the *Marauding Elephant*.

Of course it wasn't. Finian's lads don't wear Carhartts. They are way too rock 'n' roll.

"The *Hellraiser's* a claim-jumper," Ruby goes on. "They explored Suckass, found the A-tech, stashed it on board their ship … Basically the same shit happened to them as happened to us. But listen, Fletch, they got the A-tech under control in time. Their ship is still spaceworthy."

Yes, I know, I think to myself. Last seen chopping up the *Marauding Elephant* with its broadside lasers.

"*But!* Their stacker got chomped. So they can't get back on the Railroad. And they're running out of consumables. They're desperate, man. So I made a deal with them. We give them Penelope to operate their ship, and in return they take us out of here. Are you listening, Fletch?"

I am, but I'm also listening to the faint sound of voices from inside the control room. The walls are as thin as paper on this ship. It sounds like Penelope's taking to someone in there.

"Not a bad plan," I say, and that's when an avalanche of anti-grav gadgets falls down the hatchway, followed by Donal and Sakashvili.

"He coming!" Sakashvili shouts. "He escape from mess!"

Sakashvili frantically climbs back up the ladder with one of our anti-grav cargo dollies. It's a sheet of plastic with an anti-grav engine underneath and collapsible rails on top. We're trying to wedge it into the hatch at the top of the ladder when I smell the choking odor of musty fur.

"Penny!" shouts Donal, oblivious. "It's me!"

The control room door hisses open and there stands Penelope in an unusual costume, for her, of a Brown University t-shirt and sweatpants.

And there stands Harriet at her side, only she's not so much standing as struggling on her tippy-toes, because Penelope has a metalforma knife hovering at her throat.

These knives are the business. They grow on contact, sending out nasty little spikes and tendrils, so even the smallest wound is likely to kill. A-tech. Of course.

"You have to make a choice," Penelope announces. "Her or me? Which is it to be, Donal?"

"You can't do this," Donal husks weakly. "I mean, I order you to release her!"

"Huh," Penelope sneers. "You suck at dominance." Her voice trembles with self-pity. "I really know how to pick 'em."

Up in the corridor, Mama-zilla can smell all the lovely electricity coursing through the equipment in the control room. Her wingbeats throb like a jet engine. Dark wing-points shoot around the edges of the dolly. I whack at them with an anti-grav tea tray.

My life has now officially reached peak embuggerment.

Well, at least it isn't raining.

Two seconds later it starts to rain … flame-retardant foam.

The fire in the kitchen must have triggered the sprinklers.

The foam falls straight through Mama-Zilla's wing-points, making them glow gray. If chronic depression had a color this would be it. These fluttering points of existential misery wrap around the edges of the anti-grav dolly and embrace Sakashvili.

His biohazard suit doesn't give him enough protection. He crumples. His falling body knocks me off the ladder.

I land on the heap of EVA suits, slip in the foam, and catch myself—pure reflex, I promise—on Penelope's legs.

She staggers back into the control room, taking Harriet with her.

Donal is still rooted to the spot. But clever Harriet seizes her chance. While Penelope's off balance, Harriet bites her ear.

Penelope yowls and drops her knife. Metalforma is wasted on amateurs.

I charge into the control room, catch Penelope with my shoulder, and knock her to the floor.

Harriet starts to run to Donal, then backpedals at the sight of Mama-zilla.

The A-tech horror heaves through the door and into the control room with us, wings spreading to all four walls, quivering as if it can't decide what to eat first, now that it's surrounded by such bounty. It settles on the flight control computers.

The lights dim. Various background hums fade to silence as the *Skint Idjit* suffers an unscheduled power-down.

When it has finished with the ship it will eat us. By that time, I expect EVA suits will pose no obstacle to it.

And then it will move on to eat another hole in the Interstellar Railroad … just like the ones off the *Hellraiser* did before.

And maybe the gandy dancers'll be able to stop it this time, or maybe they won't, and maybe it'll eat the entire Railroad from one end of the Milky Way to the other.

And maybe that'd be a good thing.

But on the whole, I think not.

Penelope, on the floor, is crawling under her bed to get away from the monster.

Her *anti-grav* bed, which I have seen her fly around the leafy suburbs of Treetop like a flitter, with Donal behind her holding onto her shoulders and the both of them screeching like kids on a rollercoaster, in the days when things were good.

I close the visor of my helmet. Almost immediately I start to suffocate.

I take a flying leap, *through* Mama-zilla's miserable wings, and land on the bed. Where are the bloody controls?

Ah, here.

I power the bed up to the ceiling, yank it into position, and then force it down.

Right on top of Mama-zilla.

Unfortunately Penelope's under there, too.

CHAPTER 15

The weaponized bed didn't kill Mama-zilla, but it gave her pause for thought. That was long enough for Penelope to dive out of the way. She brushed Mama-zilla's wings and hit the floor looking rather gray. The bright side is she's no longer in any shape to threaten us. It's all she can do to struggle into her own high-end EVA suit and flee the ship, helped along by Donal and Harriet, whose capacity for forgiveness astounds me.

Final headcount of survivors: twelve. Six South Africans. One assistant propulsion tech (her name turns out to be Vanessa). Donal. Harriet. Penelope. And Ruby and me.

The others have scattered over the surface of the planetary shard. I can't see them anymore, and we've got no radio contact with them.

Ruby's hanging onto my belt. He's totally dependent on me to guide him, as his visor is now a mass of duct tape.

"I don't see the *Hellraiser*," I tell him.

Our shard has tumbled around on its axis and we're now facing away from Planet No.27's sun. In the abyss of space 'above' us float angular bits of rubble lit up like the moon. The local loop, also lit up, encircles the horizon like a thin silver rainbow. This is how it looks from Earth at night, if you get out into the countryside. It's a beautiful view, and strikingly empty of ships.

"The *Hellraiser's* gotta be there, man! They told me they'd wait for me to bring Penelope! Anyway, where would they go?"

Ruby and I are talking to each other by radio. I made sure to get a spare powerpack off him as soon as the others were out of sight.

"Oh, I dunno," I say. "But like I said, we don't really need Penelope, do we?"

"What do you mean?"

"You're a stacker yourself, aren't you, Ruby?"

"I, uh, no. Nope. Well … kinda. Yeah, I guess."

He admits it. I smirk to myself. The truth dawned on me after I met Finian's stackers. They don't have to look like it. And anyway, Ruby works for Goldman Sachs. The possibility was there all along.

"But that doesn't mean I can operate a ship! There *is* training involved."

"I'm sure you'll be able to pick it up as you go along. You're a smart guy."

He laughs weakly. "Damn, I was *so* hoping to get out of this. I'm just sick of it, you know? Do as you're told, go where you're sent, make your quota or lose your bonus …Being a stacker means you're never free. You people don't know how good you have it."

"Nobody forced you at gunpoint to work for Goldman Sachs," I point out.

"No, but if you graduate from Harvard, what else are you gonna do? And then you wind up fetching the boss's goddamn coffee, and then they send me all the way out here to spy on some kooky exploration activist's sex life, like I'm a fucking PI or something. I can't take it anymore."

Jesus, the self-pity. I recognize it because it could have been me a few weeks ago, only with different complaints. Self-pity isn't a stacker monopoly.

"So, OK." He heaves a sigh. "I guess donating my brainpower to a bunch of pirates … it's better than a poke in the eye with a sharp stick."

"I'm glad you feel that way," I say.

The beep-beep-beep of my suit's radar homing guidance has sped up. Hauling Ruby with me, I fly over a jagged cliff and there's the *Marauding Elephant*.

A space toboggan zips towards us, a rotund black-clad figure atop it.

"Meet my uncle Finian," I say to Ruby. "I'm sure the two of you will get along great."

CHAPTER 16

"We captured her in fifteen minutes flat," my uncle tells me, showing us around the ship formerly known as the *Hellraiser.* "It was a cakewalk." He seems a bit aggrieved about that. "There were only two people on board."

"Two!" marvels Harriet.

"Yes, the captain and the pilot, may their souls rest in peace, or not as the case may be. They'd locked themselves in the bridge."

"To escape the Butterfly-zillas?"

"No, this would have been later. It looks as if they jettisoned all the A-tech right after they came off the Railroad. But it had already cut a swathe through them. Their stacker was dead. Which is why you should *always* have a back-up ... but they didn't. So they were stuck." Of course, I've already heard this from Ruby, who was plotting to un-stick the *Hellraiser* with my help. "That was five months ago, according to the pilot," my uncle goes on. "Five *months!* So you can imagine."

"I'm surprised even two of them managed to live that long," Harriet says innocently.

"We've tidied the place up for you," Finian says, seemingly changing the subject. He waves at the large, barren mess. I know what he's talking about because I helped with the tidying up before the others came on board. There were ... *bones*.

"What happened to the captain?" Donal says.

"He ate his gun," Finian says curtly.

The former *Hellraiser* is indeed an F-99. Those military boys love their grey paint, ugly strip lighting, and touch screens on every blessed thing (all broken now). Subsequent owners have tweaked the ambiance with classic rap posters and rude graffiti.

Vanessa and Harriet gaze around disconsolately. "I wish *I'd* gone on the *Elephant,*" Vanessa sighs.

She is alluding to Penelope, who's currently in the *Elephant's* sick-bay. It was the only place for her after her encounter with Mama-zilla. If she wasn't a stacker, she'd probably have died, like Morgan did, but those drugs they take enhance their powers of recuperation into the bargain. They're going to have a lively old time of it on the *Elephant*, I reckon. On the other hand, I wouldn't be at all surprised if one of Finian's crew turned out to be into BDSM.

"*I* don't wish I'd gone on the *Elephant,*" Harriet says, smiling at Donal. He takes her hand, pulls her close, and kisses her.

Vanessa scoops up a treecat and kisses that. "Well, at least we've got the kitties."

Harriet and Vanessa actually went back to the *Skint Idjit* to rescue the treecats. That's what I call courage, otherwise known as rank idiocy. There's really not much difference. The treecats now have the run of the *Hellraiser's* crew deck. They've been piddling everywhere. It's a good thing they're so damn cute.

For all the mass of the ship, the interior is pretty cramped, but we're used to that. And anyway there are only eleven of us now.

Our tour ends on the bridge, where the last survivor of the *Hellraiser* is cringing on the pilot's couch, guarded by Adriaan and Shaka, two of our South Africans. The pilot may have a pirate's hedgehog haircut and metallic tattoos, but he's been the most cooperative of captives, as you would be in his position. Anyway, his name is Kenneth. I can't imagine someone named Kenneth killing us all in a suicidal act of revenge. And if he should try it, I'll just grab the controls.

"Well, I've got to get on," says my uncle, picking up his elephant-tusked helmet. "Oh, by the way, Fletcher, I think this is yours?"

He reaches into his spacesuit's thigh pocket and holds out my lightsaber.

I goggle, too surprised to move. I thought that was lost forever, back on the *Skint Idjit.*

Finian checks that no one else is close enough to overhear, and murmurs, "Your man had it with him in his rucksack." No one else knows that Ruby is safe and sound on board the *Marauding Elephant,* and we would both like it to stay that way.

"That little prick," I mutter through clenched teeth.

"Well, do you want it?"

I hesitate.

Finian reads my hesitation accurately. I stole it off him twenty years ago, according to him; why is he giving it back to me now?

"Oh," he says, "I figure you've earned it. You got the job done back there." He winks.

"Ta," is all I can think of to say, sliding the lightsaber into my pocket.

Hoping to hell I never have to use it again.

Everyone says goodbye and thank you to Finian. "I'll look

forward to buying you a drink at O'Donoghue's in the not too distant future," Donal says. Finian makes noncommittal noises, and flies back to his ship.

Both ships are now standing off—*well* off—from the shard where the *Skint Idjit* is lodged.

We can't actually see the *Idjit* anymore. But infrared scans reveal a patch of warmth at her location. It flutters.

I think we have solved the mystery of what destroyed Planet No. 27, incidentally. There's a lot of heat energy in a planet.

A normally rotating planet, that is.

Not so much on the nightside of a tidally locked planet. Which is why unnamed aliens, billions of years ago, must have thought it would make a good cold storage locker.

Well, I'm not so sure about that. But I do know that these shards are not a safe place for Mama-zilla and her family. They *move*.

So, after the *Marauding Elephant* has zoomed off up the Railroad, Donal gives a command: "Acquire target."

"Target acquired," says Shaka, who has been pining for years to get his hands on some guns like the former *Hellraiser's*.

"Ready missiles."

"Missiles ready."

"Fire!"

With a boom that catches us all by surprise, the F-99 unloads her twin dorsal railguns. Kinetic projectiles, *not* energy beams, streak through space and smash into the shard where Mama-zilla is digesting its meal. Megatons of shrapnel spurt into space.

This was my idea, based on swatting the Baby-zillas. You can smash their energy receptors or something. I hope to

God I'm right about how it works. I'm just guessing.

At any rate, when the dust drifts away, we run another infrared scan, and it does seem a bit cooler down there now.

"Poor old *Skint Idjit*," Donal says mournfully. "I never dreamed it would end this way."

"Oh, shut up," says the unsentimental Harriet. "This ship's much better."

There is no question the F-99 is a faster, bigger, more heavily armed ship than the *Skint Idjit* was. *Better* is a matter of taste, but *more valuable* is not.

"We can sell her on Arcadia and then go home," Harriet says.

I laugh out loud, knowing Donal better than that. Harriet scowls at me. "Well, what are *you* planning to do, Fletch?"

Our new stacker, Gordon, saves me from having to answer. "Might we be planning to hit the tracks any time soon?" he yawns.

Uncle Finian has lent us his back-up stacker. Gordon F. Poole is seventy-eight and sports a mustache like those old pictures of Chinese sages. He was quite happy to be lent, on the condition that he gets to work on the bridge *and* play his music, which helps him concentrate. So we are all listening to Avenged Sevenfold, and before that it was Queens of the Stone Age and something called Eagles of Death Metal, God help us.

"Oh, ah, yes," says Donal, who's a bit in awe of Gordon. "Whenever you're ready."

So we sail onto the Interstellar Railroad and accelerate painlessly to thousands of times the speed of light. Donal cracks a bottle of champagne, we drink to the memory of our dead colleagues, everyone gets emotional, Vanessa gets off with Kenneth the pirate, and Harriet completely forgets her question.

I bet you have forgotten it, too.

The question was: What am I planning to do when we reach Arcadia?

The answer is I'm not sure yet.

But I *did* recover one of the body bags full of Baby-zillas that Ruby threw out of the airlock.

And I *did* give it to Finian after I handed Ruby over to him.

And Finian left Planet No. 27 before we did, which will put him on Arcadia several days ahead of us, since we'll have to make at least one water stop en route.

As soon as he gets there, he'll announce the A-tech discovery and claim his 50%.

Only 50%? Yes. This find is too big to be auctioned off under the table. We agreed he'd better turn the Butterfly-zillas over to their rightful owners, Goldman Sachs. They might try to stiff him, since he hasn't got an exploration contract with them. But he *has* got a Goldman Sachs employee on board: Jacob Ruby, who will lie his arse off to prove Finian's claim, if he values his wretched life. And everyone can agree that 50% of untold billions is a lot better than 50% of nothing.

I'm getting 40% of Finian's 50%, which is still so much money it makes me giddy.

I might share it with Donal and the others, just to make Donal feel *really* bad.

Or I might buy a planet.

Or, I suppose, Finian might try to stiff me. But I don't think it's likely. He knows that if he did that, he'd never be able to hold up his head in Lisdoonvarna again.

THE RELUCTANT ADVENTURES
OF
FLETCHER CONNOLLY
ON THE
INTERSTELLAR RAILROAD
VOLUME 2

INTERGALACTIC BOGTROTTER

Some things call for a little payback....

Fletcher Connolly had more to lose than he thought. After the loss of the Skint Idjit, Fletch and the Idjit's crew face something far worse than the Butterfly-zillas of Suckass. In debt to Goldman Sachs to the tune of $50 million in cash, Fletch is willing to do just about anything to settle the balance.

But when Fletch is forced to swallow his pride, and take their new ship, the Intergalactic Bogtrotter, under the hiring hand of his greedy, piratical uncle, the situation spirals from desperate to outright murderous. Hit by a surprise attack and flung off the Interstellar Railroad into deep space, Fletch, Donal, and the rest of the crew wind up dead-lined on a rogue planet. With the Bogtrotter in desperate need of repair and the unstable conditions of a sunless planet threatening their survival, the crew find themselves between the cross hairs of Finian Connolly's oldest rival.

Can Fletch find a way to turn the tables on this decade-old vendetta, and revenge himself satisfactorily on his uncle?

Or will Finian's murderous grudge cost them all more than they are willing to pay?

DISCOVER THE ADVENTUROUS WORLDS OF FELIX R. SAVAGE

An exuberant storyteller with a demented imagination, Felix R. Savage specializes in creating worlds so exciting, you'll never want to leave.

Join the Savage Stories newsletter to get notified of new releases and chances to win free books. As a subscriber's gift, you'll also get a free copy of *Rubbish With Names,* the prequel to the Interstellar Railroad series!

http://felixrsavage.com/updates

THE RELUCTANT ADVENTURES

OF

FLETCHER CONNOLLY

ON THE

INTERSTELLAR RAILROAD

Near-Future Non-Hard Science Fiction

An Irishman in space. Untold hoards of alien technological relics waiting to be discovered. What could possibly go wrong?

Skint Idjit
Intergalactic Bogtrotter
Banjaxed Ceili
Supermassive Blackguard

THE SOL SYSTEM RENEGADES SERIES

Near-Future Hard Science Fiction

A genocidal AI is devouring our solar system. Can a few brave men and women save humanity?

In the year 2288, humanity stands at a crossroads between space colonization and extinction. Packed with excitement, heartbreak, and unforgettable characters, the Sol System Renegades series tells a sweeping tale of struggle and deliverance.

Crapkiller
The Galapagos Incident
The Vesta Conspiracy
The Mercury Rebellion
The Luna Deception
The Phobos Maneuver
The Mars Shock
The Callisto Gambit
Keep Off The Grass (short story)
A Very Merry Zero-Gravity Christmas (short story)

FIRST CONTACT, INC.

Not A User's Manual

The alien rulers of the galaxy are pyramid marketers, and humanity's role in the grand scam is to play the sucker at the bottom.

Unless we can find suckers of our own to prey on ...

Against The Rules
Payback

Made in United States
Orlando, FL
31 December 2021

12710503R00068